"Mom, why don't you like Patrick's dad?" Missy asked.

Shelley sighed. "I don't dislike Mr. Taylor, honey. He's just not a person I feel comfortable with."

"But why not?" Missy pressed. "He's *really* nice. I like him a *lot!*"

"I'm glad you do, honey," Shelley returned. She fervently hoped Missy would drop the subject of John Taylor.

"I wish you liked him," Missy resumed. "If you and Patrick's dad were friends, then we could all do things together. That would be *so* much fun."

Warning bells went off in Shelley's mind.

Might Missy be trying to matchmake?

But Shelley immediately dismissed the idea. It was too farfetched.

After all, what would a little girl know about matchmaking?

Dear Reader,

Brides, babies and families...that's just what Special Edition has in store for you this August! All this and more from some of your favorite authors.

Our THAT'S MY BABY! title for this month is *Of Texas Ladies, Cowboys...and Babies*, by popular Silhouette Romance author Jodi O'Donnell. In her first book for Special Edition, Jodi tells of a still young and graceful grandmother-to-be who unexpectedly finds herself in the family way! Fans of Jodi's latest Romance novel, *Daddy Was a Cowboy*, won't want to miss this spin-off title!

This month, GREAT EXPECTATIONS, the wonderful new series of family and homecoming by Andrea Edwards, continues with *A Father's Gift*. And summer just wouldn't be right without a wedding, so we present *A Bride for John*, the second book of Trisha Alexander's newest series, THREE BRIDES AND A BABY. Beginning this month is a new miniseries from veteran author Pat Warren, REUNION. Three siblings must find each other as they search for true love. It all begins with one sister's story in *A Home for Hannah*.

Also joining the Special Edition family this month is reader favorite and Silhouette Romance author Stella Bagwell. Her first title for Special Edition is *Found: One Runaway Bride*. And returning to Special Edition this August is Carolyn Seabaugh with *Just a Family Man*, as the lives of one woman and her son are forever changed when an irresistible man walks into their café in the wild West.

This truly is a month packed with summer fun and romance! I hope you enjoy each and every story to come!

Sincerely,
Tara Gavin, Senior Editor

Please address questions and book requests to:
Silhouette Reader Service
U.S.: 3010 Walden Ave., P.O. Box 1325, Buffalo, NY 14269
Canadian: P.O. Box 609, Fort Erie, Ont. L2A 5X3

TRISHA ALEXANDER

A BRIDE FOR JOHN

SPECIAL EDITION®

Published by Silhouette Books
America's Publisher of Contemporary Romance

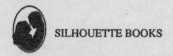

SILHOUETTE BOOKS

ISBN 0-373-24047-3

A BRIDE FOR JOHN

This edition published by arrangement with Harlequin Books S.A.

® and TM are trademarks of Harlequin Books S.A., used under license.
Trademarks indicated with ® are registered in the United States Patent
and Trademark Office, the Canadian Trade Marks Office and in other
countries.

Printed in U.S.A.

Books by Trisha Alexander

Silhouette Special Edition

Cinderella Girl #640
When Somebody Loves You #748
When Somebody Needs You #784
Mother of the Groom #801
When Somebody Wants You #822
Here Comes the Groom #845
Say You Love Me #875
What Will the Children Think? #906
Let's Make It Legal #924
The Real Elizabeth Hollister... #940
The Girl Next Door #965
This Child Is Mine #989
A Bride for Luke #1024
A Bride for John #1047

*Three Brides and a Baby

TRISHA ALEXANDER

has had a lifelong love affair with books and has always wanted to be a writer. She also loves cats, movies, the ocean, music, Broadway shows, cooking, traveling, being with her family and friends, Cajun food, Calvin and Hobbes and getting mail. Trisha and her husband have three grown children, three adorable grandchildren and live in Houston, Texas. Trisha loves to hear from readers. You can write to her at P.O. Box 441603, Houston, TX 77244-1603.

The Taylor Family

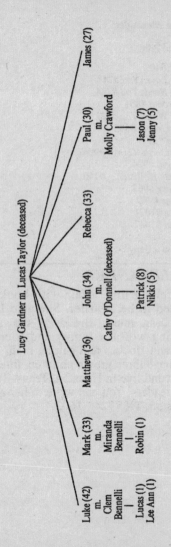

Lucy Gardner m. Lucas Taylor (deceased)

Luke (42)
m.
Clem
Bennelli

Lucas (1)
Lee Ann (1)

Mark (33)
m.
Miranda
Bennelli

Robin (1)

Matthew (36)

John (34)
m.
Cathy O'Donnell (deceased)

Patrick (8)
Nikki (5)

Rebecca (33)

Paul (30)
m.
Molly Crawford

Jason (7)
Jenny (5)

James (27)

Prologue

"Patrick, can I ask you something?"

Patrick Taylor, age eight, glanced up at his best friend, Missy Broome, who would soon be eight, and wondered why she looked so serious. "Sure."

It was a hot Saturday in September, and the two friends were sitting inside Missy's tree house, reading X-men comic books and eating Doritos and M&M's.

Patrick liked the tree house better than any place, because it sat high up in the big black willow tree that shaded Missy's backyard. In the winter it was snug and warm, and in the summer it was cool, but the best part was, it was their own private spot, and no one could see them or spy on them when they were in it.

"Do you miss your mom?"

A funny, achy feeling stole into Patrick's stomach. He swallowed, nodding his head. "Yeah," he answered softly. "I miss her a lot."

They were both quiet for a while, then Missy said, "I miss having a dad around, too."

Patrick started to say that your parents being divorced wasn't the same as your mother dying, but he didn't. Instead he nodded again and waited. Missy had something on her mind. Patrick could always tell.

Sure enough, a few seconds later she said, "I was thinking..."

"What about?"

"Well, you miss your mom, and I miss having a dad around, and you told me your dad has been really sad since your mom died..."

"Yeah," Patrick said guardedly.

Her earnest little face suddenly broke into a smile. "Well, wouldn't it be neat if we could get your dad and my mom together?"

Patrick frowned. "Together?" he repeated. "Like how?"

"Oh, c'mon, Patrick, don't be *stupid!* You know like how. Like married to each other."

"*Married* to each other?" Patrick squeaked. "They don't even *like* each other!"

He and Missy had discussed their parents' obvious antagonism many times, because even though Missy and her mom had lived across the street from Patrick and his dad for more than five years now, and even though Missy and Patrick were best friends, for some reason his dad and her mom did not get along.

Missy's mom pretended she liked Patrick's dad, but Missy and Patrick both knew better because Missy had overheard her mom telling her best friend that Patrick's dad was a stuffed shirt, and Missy and Patrick had looked up the term in the dictionary. When Patrick had realized Missy's mom was calling his dad smug and conceited, he'd known for sure that she didn't like his dad at all.

And Patrick's dad had said to Patrick many times how he thought if Missy's mom spent half as much time with Missy as she did on her job, maybe Missy wouldn't look like such a ragamuffin. Patrick wanted to know what a ragamuffin was, and his dad said, "Oh, forget it. It's none of our business."

"Yeah," Missy said. "It'd be perfect. Then you and me, we'd almost be brother and sister, and we could all live in the same house together, and you'd have a mom, and I'd have a dad." She broke off, giving Patrick a sharp look. "*You* like my mom, don't you?"

"Heck, yeah," Patrick said without hesitation. "I think she's neat."

"And I *love* your dad!" Missy said enthusiastically.

Patrick knew this was true. Missy had told him many times how much she wished she had a dad like his instead of the dad she had, because her dad hardly ever called her now that he'd moved to Colorado with his new wife and they had a new baby and all.

It always made Patrick feel bad when Missy talked like that, because at least he knew his mom had loved him and she hadn't left him because she wanted to, but because she'd gotten so sick.

"So what do you say?" Missy said. "Wanna see if we can come up with a plan?"

"But I don't see how we can make 'em *like* each other if they don't."

"They just don't know each other, that's all," Missy said. "All we have to do is figure out a way to get 'em together."

Patrick wasn't so sure it would be that easy, but he hated to say so, mainly because once Missy got something in her head, it was almost impossible to change her mind. Once, when he'd told his dad this, his dad had laughed and said, "Typical woman!"

Patrick sighed. "Well, I guess we could try."

Missy smiled.

"How should we start?" Patrick asked.

"Well, you know my birthday's in two weeks."

"Uh-huh."

"And my mom said just yesterday that she'd let me invite two friends to go to Astroworld with me."

"Awesome!" Patrick said, punching his fist in the air. He hadn't been to Astroworld this year at all and he was dying to go.

"Well, how about if I ask you and your dad?"

Patrick grimaced. "Your mom'll get mad."

Missy shrugged. "Maybe, but she's not gonna be rude and tell him he can't go, not after I've invited him, is she?"

"I don't know," Patrick said doubtfully.

"Even if she's mad, she'll still have to spend the day with us," Missy pointed out. "And if your dad and my mom are together all day and ride on the rides together and everything, they're *sure* to end up liking each other."

Patrick wasn't as sure as Missy that things would turn out the way she'd described, but he knew, when she had that stubborn tilt to her chin and that I'm-gonna-do-this look in her eyes, it was useless for him to protest. Plus, he really, really wanted to go to Astroworld. "Well," he said slowly, "if you think so..."

In answer, Missy only grinned happily.

After a few seconds, Patrick grinned, too.

Chapter One

Shelley Broome felt like crying. Some days it simply didn't pay to get up in the morning, and this was one of them.

As if it weren't bad enough that she'd overslept, which meant Missy would be late for school, and that it was raining buckets, which meant Houston's streets would be flooded in exactly the places Shelley needed to go this morning, and that one of her three cats had thrown up all over the living room carpet—now Mrs. Dunbar, her sitter, had called saying she had the flu, which meant she couldn't watch Missy after school today or tomorrow.

Shelley wondered aloud what else could go wrong. "What did I do to deserve this?" she muttered.

"Chill out, Mom," Missy said, busily spreading peanut butter on wheat bread. "You know it's not good for your stomach to get upset." Her gray eyes, the exact shade of Shelley's, were filled with old-soul wisdom.

Shelley gave her nearly eight-year-old daughter a baleful look. "I can't help it. I'm in a real bind. Tonight's okay. I don't have any appointments this afternoon, so I can leave early. But tomorrow's impossible. I've been trying to get Mrs. Van Doren out to look at houses for two weeks now, and she's finally cleared her calendar and given me all day tomorrow, and now Mrs. Dunbar's cancelled...." Shelley could feel a headache coming on, which didn't bode well for the rest of the day.

"It's okay," Missy said. "I can go to Patrick's house tomorrow. His dad won't care."

Shelley grimaced. Patrick Taylor's dad was one of her least favorite people. Maybe John Taylor *wouldn't* mind watching Missy tomorrow, but Shelley would mind asking him. The last time she'd asked him to pinch hit for her baby-sitter, he'd made a remark that Shelley hadn't liked, implying that her daughter's welfare was more important than her job and maybe she should rethink her priorities.

Easy for John Taylor to say, she'd thought resentfully. He worked in his family's security business. If he had to stay home with a sick child or for any other personal reason, he didn't incur the wrath of anyone nor did he jeopardize his job.

Shelley didn't have that luxury. In fact, Shelley and Missy didn't have any luxuries at all. That was one of the reasons Shelley had worked so hard to get her real estate license. So she would be able to take better care of Missy and give her some of the advantages children like Patrick Taylor had.

One of the things Shelley especially wanted to do for Missy was give her gymnastics lessons. Missy showed so much promise in gymnastics, as her physical education teacher had told Shelley several times. *Soon,* Shelley promised herself, *soon.* All she really had to do was sell Mrs. Van Doren a house—a nice, big house that would pay a nice, big commission.

"I'll ask Patrick about tomorrow when I see him in school," Missy said. She stuffed her sandwich into a plastic sandwich bag, then shoved it into her lunch box, where it joined a Granny Smith apple, two Fig Newtons, and carrot sticks.

Shelley often wondered how she had ever managed to conceive a child like Missy. Missy was organized, logical, and mature in ways that constantly amazed Shelley. What other seven-year-old made sure she not only had fruit but fresh vegetables in her lunch? None whom Shelley knew.

"Okay?" Missy said, closing her lunch box.

"Oh, all right, I guess so. Go ahead and ask him." Although Shelley would have preferred finding another sitter, she knew Missy loved being at Patrick's house, and Missy's happiness was more important than Shelley's pride. Besides, if John agreed to let Missy spend the day tomorrow, Shelley would insist on reciprocating. Fair was fair. "Now let's get going. Maybe I can get you to school before the tardy bell rings."

Ten minutes later Shelley pulled under the covered entrance to Missy's school, leaned over to kiss Missy goodbye, then waved as her daughter's red-slicker-clad body disappeared through the double glass doors.

Shelley sighed as she pulled out into the downpour and drove to her office located ten miles away on Memorial Drive near Town and Country Shopping Center. She hoped there were no other disasters lurking around the corner today. She was about all disastered out.

John Taylor sat at his desk and stared at the white figures on the blue computer screen in front of him. Since his sister Rebecca had bailed out of Taylor Security two years ago, John had taken over the number crunching for the family's business.

He'd been glad to leave field work behind. He'd never really been cut out for it. Maybe if he hadn't had a wife he adored and two kids he wanted to be around for, he might have enjoyed the travel and danger associated with the security business.

And now that he'd lost Cathy, it was even more imperative that he be there for his children and not take any needless risks. He didn't want his kids growing up both motherless and fatherless.

He sighed. God, he missed Cathy. It had been nearly three years since she'd succumbed to a virulent strain of leukemia, but the missing hadn't gotten any easier. They'd had such a good marriage. Against all odds, too. His smile was bittersweet as he remembered how the two of them had enjoyed showing everyone they were wrong, that a teenage marriage *could* work if the parties involved were mature enough and willing enough to work hard at it.

Oh, Cathy, Cathy...why did this have to happen to us? I need you. The kids need you....

If he closed his eyes, he could see her perfectly, could almost imagine her presence in the office with him. Her bouncy dark hair, her equally dark eyes filled with laughter, her curvy little body that he'd never tired of looking at...or making love to.

Swallowing hard, he forced the images away. He couldn't afford to indulge in these fits of self-pity and let's-pretend. He had two wonderful kids at home who needed him to be strong. Two kids who needed him to provide a safe, secure, happy environment. Two kids who were more important to him than anything else in the world.

He would never let them down.

Just as the vow formed, the phone at his elbow rang. He picked it up automatically.

"John Taylor."

"Dad?"

John grinned. He'd recognize the voice of his eight-year-old anywhere. "Hi, Patrick." John glanced at the clock. It was three thirty-four. "What're you doing home so early? I thought you had soccer practice."

"It got cancelled 'cause of the rain."

"Oh, of course. Well, what's up? You need something?"

"No, I just wanted to ask you something."

"Okay."

"Can Missy go to the zoo with us tomorrow?"

John frowned. "Now, Patrick, I thought we agreed the trip to the zoo was going to be strictly a family outing."

"I know, Dad," Patrick said earnestly, "but her mom has to work, and the baby-sitter can't come, and Missy doesn't want to stay with anyone else."

Irritation sidled through John. He really liked Missy, but that mother of hers was another story. John had done his best to avoid contact with Shelley since Cathy's death. Shelley and Cathy had been best friends almost from the moment they'd met, something that had always puzzled John, because no two women could have been more different. He had expressed his reservations about Shelley several times, and each time Cathy would gently reprove him, saying he just didn't know Shelley well enough. "She's a wonderful person, John, truly."

He'd remained unconvinced. He thought Shelley had a chip on her shoulder. He also thought she was subtly trying to change Cathy, that she thought Cathy was too much under his influence, and that really irritated John. Cathy had made her own choices in life. If those choices happened to be John's preferences, that was because he and his wife were united in their beliefs and goals.

His biggest problem with Shelley right now was that he thought she was more concerned with making it big in her career than with providing the proper kind of homelife for Missy.

He knew Shelley had to work. After all, she was a single parent. But why had she opted for a profession where her most lucrative hours would be those when Missy was not in school? Surely there were any number of other professions she could have chosen that would enable her to spend more time with Missy.

Even the way Shelley looked irritated him. Cool blondes with frosty gray eyes and tall, thin frames simply were not his cup of tea.

"Please, Dad?"

John opened his mouth to refuse, then thought about what a sweet kid Missy was and how her father neglected her. Why was he taking his disapproval of Shelley out on Missy? Was it really such a big deal to have her go along with them tomorrow? She'd be company for Patrick, and even for Nikki, his five-year-old, who had a bad case of hero worship where Missy was concerned.

"Oh, all right, Patrick. All right. Missy can come with us."

"Gee, thanks, Dad!"

"You're welcome. Now, would you please tell Aunt Froggie I want to talk to her?"

"Sure, Dad. Aunt Frog-*geeeeeee!* Dad's on the phone!"

John winced and held the receiver away from his ear.

A few seconds later, Mary Margaret Phrogge, Cathy's aunt and John's live-in baby-sitter, housekeeper, and valued friend and ally, said, "Hello, John."

"Hi, Froggie. Everything under control there?"

"As under control as it's possible to be with these two," she said affectionately.

"What's Nikki doing?"

"Still napping. She was worn-out from preschool today. They must have played really hard."

"Nikki always plays hard."

"I know. I wish I had just half her energy."

"And I wish I had just half of yours. Listen, I thought I might pick up some pizza on the way home. Save you from cooking."

"Too late. I've got a casserole ready to put in the oven. Besides, pizza is loaded with fat."

John smiled. Froggie was one in a million. She not only watched his kids and his house, she watched John's cholesterol and his weight and worried about his lack of a social life. "Okay, Mom," he teased. "I'll see you about five-thirty."

He was still smiling after he hung up and turned his attention back to the computer and the spreadsheet he'd been working on when Patrick called.

Froggie had saved his life after Cathy died. She had stepped in and taken over and was as devoted to him and his children as if she were their grandmother instead of their great-aunt. He knew he was lucky to have her. Various friends complained enough about their own baby-sitting problems for John to know he was extremely fortunate.

His thoughts naturally segued to Shelley Broome and her child-care problems. He felt vaguely guilty for his earlier thoughts. Maybe he was being too hard on the woman. After all, not everyone could have a Froggie in their lives. Still...it seemed to him that Missy's mother should make a concerted effort to find a good, reliable person to care for Missy. And if she couldn't, then she should find another job—one that didn't require so many long hours—especially so many evening and weekend hours.

The next time Shelley asked John to pinch hit for her baby-sitter, he might say just that.

*   *   *

Shelley looked at the clock mounted on her car's dash. Oh, God, it was three forty-five! Missy would already be home. And here Shelley was, stuck on the Loop in some kind of horrible bottleneck of traffic that had come to a complete standstill.

She reached for her car phone and punched in her home number. The answering machine kicked in, and after the message played through, Shelley said, "Missy? It's me, Mom. If you're there, pick up."

"Hi, Mom."

"Sugar, listen, I'm really sorry, but I'm stuck in traffic. There's some kind of accident or something. I don't know when I'm going to get there."

"Oh. Okay."

It *wasn't* okay, and Shelley knew it. Missy might be mature for her age, but she was still only seven, and she didn't like being home alone, even though she pretended not to mind. Shelley didn't *want* her home alone, even though Missy had a house key taped inside her lunch box just in case. "Now remember, keep the door locked, and don't answer the phone, and don't go anywhere. You've got my car phone number, so you can call me if you need me for anything. Okay?"

"Okay."

"I'm sorry, honey."

"I know, Mom."

"And I'll get there as fast as I can."

"Okay."

"Damn!" Shelley said after they hung up. "Damn, damn, damn!" This was one of the most horrible days of her life, and it wasn't over yet. She craned her neck to see if she could figure out what the holdup was, but all she saw were four lanes of red brake lights.

Added to the frustration of sitting in the traffic mess was the niggling worry about Missy being alone. *Nothing will happen to her,* Shelley told herself. She'll be fine.

Ten minutes later, having crept a few hundred yards, Shelley had gained the top of a small rise and could finally see ahead. She groaned. Several sets of flashing lights told her there was a major accident. No telling how long she'd be stuck.

Just as she considered whether she should call Missy again, the car phone buzzed.

She snatched it up. "Hello?"

"Mom?"

"Missy? Is something wrong?"

"No, Mom, I'm fine. But I called Patrick and when I told him I was by myself he asked me to come over to watch *The Lion King* with them, so I'm at his house. That's okay, isn't it?"

"Missy, you weren't supposed to leave the house!"

"I know, Mom, but I didn't think you'd care if I was at Patrick's."

"The fact remains that I told you not to leave the house, and you disobeyed me."

"I'm sorry, Mom," Missy said in a small voice, "but I didn't like being in the house by myself. And his Aunt Froggie doesn't care."

Shelley immediately felt guilty. Why was she angry with Missy? Missy was just a little kid. "It's okay. I'm sorry, too. Go watch your movie. But would you ask Patrick's aunt to come to the phone?" Shelley wouldn't have cared if Missy were at the Taylors' house if Cathy had still been alive. Cathy had always been willing to help Shelley out. In fact, she'd insisted Shelley use her, saying more times than Shelley could count that that's what friends were for. Shelley swallowed around the lump in her throat. Oh, God, she missed Cathy so much. She had been the best friend Shelley had ever had—the most caring, generous woman in the world.

"Hello?" Patrick's aunt said, jolting Shelley from her thoughts.

"Oh, hi, Mrs. Phrogge. Is it really all right for Missy to be there? I'm stuck in a terrible traffic jam on the Loop. There's been an awful accident, but I'll come get her as soon as I can."

"Don't worry about it, Shelley. It's no problem. Missy's a doll, and anyway, Patrick invited her to come over." She chuckled. "And would you please call me Froggie? Mrs. Phrogge makes me sound like a toad or something!"

Shelley laughed and thanked the older woman profusely and prayed she'd make it home before John arrived. She could just imagine the dark look of disapproval she'd get from him. She couldn't handle it, not tonight, not when Missy was going to be spending the day with him and his children tomorrow because of Shelley's baby-sitting problem.

Shelley had had about all the disapproval one woman could take in one lifetime. Starting with her parents, who were so enamored of and dazzled by Shelley's older sister, Suzanne, they didn't even know Shelley was alive, and ending with a husband who criticized everything she did, said, and thought, Shelley wondered how she'd managed to survive with any sense of self-worth at all.

It hadn't been easy.

She hadn't been able to afford counseling, which she knew would have helped her immensely, so she'd had to build her self-confidence on her own. Her first step to recovery had been her divorce. Her second had been standing up to Barry during the haggling preceding the final decree. And her third had been getting her real estate license.

In the process, she'd decided she would no longer tolerate negative influences in her life, in particular people who made her feel bad about herself. And if she *had* to deal with them, she would deal with them on her own terms. She would hold her head high, make no apologies, and she would never let them see anything other than a calm, cool, controlled woman who was just as good as they were.

Remembering, she sat up a little straighter. "Look out, world, this isn't a good day to mess with me! And that means you, too, John Taylor!"

John finished up earlier than he'd expected, so he was on his way home by four-fifteen and pulling into his driveway a few minutes after four-thirty.

The September day had turned out to be pretty once the storm had passed through, with cooler temperatures than they'd had in months. He stood outside for a minute, admiring the baby mums in the front flower beds of his two-story, redbrick Colonial home. Cathy had planted them that last spring before she got sick. She'd loved flowers of all kinds. Unfortunately, now that she wasn't around to tend them, some had died

off or were so choked with weeds they no longer
looked the way they were supposed to.

John felt guilty when he looked around, as if he'd
somehow let Cathy down because he hadn't been able
to keep her flowers fresh and beautiful. He really
should hire a good yardman to come in and whip the
yard into shape.

Deciding that's exactly what he would do, he headed
toward the back door. Good food smells greeted him
as he entered the kitchen. He smiled as he saw the
cooling apple pie on the counter.

After depositing his jacket and briefcase in his bedroom, he headed toward the TV room. There he found
his kids—and Missy Broome—sprawled on the floor
watching a Disney video. Froggie was curled up on the
couch with a magazine. She smiled in welcome as the
kids chorused their hellos.

"Hi, Mr. Taylor," Missy piped after he'd greeted
Patrick and Nikki.

"Hi, Missy."

"Her mother got stuck in a traffic jam, so Patrick
invited Missy to watch a video with us until her mom
gets home," Froggie explained.

*What the hell would the woman do if I wasn't
around?* John thought. But he kept his voice and expression pleasant.

"We're watching *The Lion King,* Daddy," Nikki
said in her sweet baby voice that always melted John's
heart.

"I can see that, cutie. Now where's my welcome-
home kiss?"

Nikki, a miniature version of her mother with her sparkly dark eyes and curly brown hair, ducked her head and grinned.

He crooked a finger at her.

She scrambled up and raced into his outstretched arms. John held her close for a long minute before releasing her to rejoin the others.

"Do you mind if I go change my clothes before you leave?" he asked Froggie. He knew tonight was her bowling night, and she always met some of her friends for an early dinner beforehand.

She smiled. "Of course not. You go ahead. I don't have to leave until five-thirty."

He walked into the hall on his way to his bedroom when, out of the corner of his eye, he saw a silver Honda turning into the driveway across the street. He hesitated. He could let Froggie answer the door, thereby avoiding having to see Shelley at all.

He gave himself a mental shake. What was wrong with him? He reversed direction and walked to the front door, watching through the side glass panel as Shelley pulled her car to a stop, opened the door, and climbed out.

He continued to watch as she slowly walked across the street and up the front sidewalk to his house. As always, she was faultlessly turned out in a gray suit paired with a pale pink blouse, gray pumps, and white stockings. Her pale hair was swept back in a chignon, and she wore understated silver jewelry.

The way she dressed was another facet of her personality that nettled him, and he couldn't have explained why. He knew her attire was appropriate for the kind of job she held and that appearances counted for a lot when a person was selling real estate.

Maybe that was it. Maybe his irritation stemmed from the fact that Shelley was obviously a career woman and that all the women he admired most were warm, motherly types who didn't get upset if a child with sticky hands hugged them or a baby spit up on them.

And maybe you resent her because she's here and Cathy isn't....

Was that it?

He didn't know. He only knew she always had this same effect on him.

Just look at her! She didn't seem at all concerned that once again he had had to step in and take over her parental responsibility. His irritation rose with each unhurried step she took. Boy, he'd like to put a dent or two in that cool armor of hers.

She had reached the front stoop by now, and she rang the doorbell. John waited a few seconds, telling himself to be pleasant. Telling himself it was not his job to give her a lesson in parenting even though she obviously needed one. Telling himself there would be a more appropriate time and a more appropriate place to discuss this situation.

He opened the door.

Shelley knew John was home because she'd seen his car in the open garage. Great, she thought. A perfect end to a perfectly rotten day. Well, no matter what he said or what kind of disapproving look he gave her, she wasn't going to let him get to her. She would thank him without groveling, she would hold her head high, and she would be coolly pleasant if it killed her.

She pressed the doorbell.

The door opened.

"Hello, Shelley," John said. His hazel eyes were devoid of warmth.

"Hello, John. Sorry about this. I got here as quickly as I could."

He nodded but he didn't smile. "Come on in."

God, would it kill him to smile? Shelley mentally shook her head as she followed him into the TV room.

"Mom! Hi!" Missy jumped up as they entered the room. She walked over to Shelley and gave her a hug.

Shelley smiled and hugged her daughter back. "Hi, sugar."

"Hi, Mrs. Broome," said Patrick, followed by the high, sweet voice of Nikki.

The kids' Aunt Froggie smiled her welcome, too, and Shelley gave the woman a warm smile in return. She really liked Froggie—a tall, spare, gray-haired woman with bright blue eyes who was probably in her late sixties.

"Does Missy have to leave now?" Patrick said, looking at John. "Can't she stay and watch the rest of the video?"

"I'm sure her mother has things she wants to do," John said stiffly.

"Yes, I do," Shelley said. He couldn't have made his feelings any clearer, she thought.

"Oh, Mrs. Broome, *please*," Patrick begged. "Can't she stay? It's okay, isn't it, Dad?"

"No," Shelley said firmly before John would be forced to reply. "She's been here long enough. Besides, she's spending the day with you tomorrow. Now come on, Missy. Gather up your things, and let's go.''

Missy didn't protest, although she shot Patrick a look that seemed to say, *grown-ups!*

After finding out what time to have Missy ready the following morning, Shelley repeated her thanks, said her goodbyes and got out of there as quickly as possible. She didn't want to spend one unnecessary minute in John Taylor's company, and it was obvious to her that he felt exactly the same way.

As she and Missy walked across the street to the house they had rented for the past five years, Shelley told herself she didn't care if John Taylor disapproved of her. He was not important in her life. What he thought didn't matter.

She vowed she would do anything she had to do to keep from being in his debt again. She would figure out a way to pay him back for tomorrow, and then, no matter what Missy said or did, no matter what emergency arose, she would not ask John Taylor for another favor.

In fact, if she never spent one more minute in his company, that would be just fine with her.

Chapter Two

"Mom," Missy said the following morning as they were both getting ready for their respective days, "why don't you like Patrick's dad?"

Shelley finished outlining her top lip with her lipstick brush before answering. "What makes you think I don't?"

Missy rolled her eyes. "'Cause you never smile when you're around him, that's why."

Shelley sighed. "I don't dislike him, honey. I just, well, he's not a person I feel comfortable with, that's all."

"But why not?" Missy pressed. "He's *really* nice. I like him a *lot!*"

"I'm glad you do, honey." Shelley returned her gaze to the mirror and added, "Now finish brushing your teeth. Patrick's dad will be here any minute to pick you up." She fervently hoped Missy would drop the subject of Shelley's feelings regarding John Taylor.

"I wish you liked him," Missy said before resuming her brushing.

Shelley didn't answer. There was no safe answer, and she wasn't about to get into her reasons for not liking John or even admitting to Missy that she didn't. She continued applying her makeup and acted as if Missy's statement didn't require a response.

Missy finished brushing her teeth and rinsed off her toothbrush. "If you and Patrick's dad were friends, then we could all do things together. That would be *so* much fun."

Warning bells went up in Shelley's mind. The thought occurred to her that Missy might be trying to matchmake. But Shelley immediately dismissed the idea. It was too farfetched to even consider. What would a little girl know about matchmaking?

No, she thought sadly, what was more likely was that Missy wanted a father. As always, when Shelley was reminded of Barry's neglect of his daughter, cold rage invaded her heart.

How *could* Barry do it? How could he practically ignore Missy's existence? Most fathers would give their eyeteeth to have a daughter like her: pretty, smart, sweet, and unselfish, too. Just an all-round wonderful kid.

Shelley still couldn't believe how he'd fooled her. She would never have predicted this kind of behavior from him when her mother had first introduced her to him. Shelley smiled grimly. Her mother had thought Barry was perfectly wonderful. She still did. Vivian Cochrane had made it perfectly clear to Shelley on numerous occasions that she blamed Shelley for the breakup of her marriage to Barry. *And* that she would never forgive her for it or let her forget about it.

"Missy," Shelley said slowly, "now is not the time to discuss this. Mr. Taylor will be here any minute. But tomorrow, I promise, we'll talk about it, okay?"

"Okay, Mom." Missy picked up one of the two barrettes laying on the vanity top.

"Here, let me do that," Shelley said. Missy's hair was just as fine and silky as Shelley's, and barrettes—unless fastened exactly right—wouldn't hold it back from her face.

"No, Mom," Missy said, resisting Shelley's effort to take the barrette away. "I can do it myself."

Shelley smothered a grin. Missy was fiercely independent about fixing her own hair and choosing her own clothes—so much so that she often looked bedraggled, but Shelley never criticized or acted as if Missy hadn't done a good job. Oh, no. Shelley'd had enough of that kind of criticism when she was growing up. She knew how it could undermine a child's self-esteem. She would never do that to Missy. Shelley firmly believed the best thing parents could do for children was show them you believed in them and thought them capable of doing anything they set their minds to. So all she said now was, "Okay."

While Missy finished putting in the barrettes, Shelley studied her. So maybe Missy's middle part was slightly off-center and a bit crooked, so what? In her red shorts and red-and-white T-shirt, paired with red socks and white sneakers and red-and-white barrettes in her blond hair, she looked cute and dressed just fine for a day at the zoo.

Shelley walked into her bedroom and found her purse. She had just given Missy a twenty-dollar bill to pay for her admission to the zoo, her lunch, and snacks, when the doorbell rang. "They're here," Shelley said.

Missy was already racing for the front door. Shelley followed behind at a more sedate pace. By the time she reached the door, Missy was already outside on the driveway. Patrick had gotten out of the car, too, but John and little Nikki were seated inside.

Shelley gave Missy a hug and kiss, then walked around to talk to John, who rolled down his window.

The morning sun gilded his face, causing his hazel eyes to sparkle and his dark hair to gleam. Not for the first time, Shelley thought what a shame it was he had the personality of a piece of wet bread, because he was really quite attractive.

"Good morning," she said in greeting. "You've got a beautiful day for the zoo."

"Yes," he agreed. "The kids are excited."

"I appreciate your taking Missy along. I know she'll have a great time."

He smiled. "No problem."

Shelley raised an inner eyebrow. He was certainly being pleasant today. He'd actually smiled! "Well, you're really helping me out, and I want to pay you back. How about if I take all the kids out to lunch and then on to Discovery Zone tomorrow afternoon?"

"Thanks, but we're expected at my mother's for dinner tomorrow."

"Oh. Well, maybe another time?"

He continued to smile, but to Shelley's eyes, the smile seemed forced. "We'll see." A heartbeat later, he added, "Three kids are a lot for one person to handle."

Shelley immediately stiffened. What was he saying? That he could manage three kids at one time but she wasn't capable of the same thing? That he didn't *trust* her to watch them? She forced herself to smile politely. "Yes, it can be a real challenge, so I'll understand if you come home early today." *Put that in your pipe and smoke it!*

He started to reply, but Nikki interrupted, saying, "Dad*deeee,* when are we gonna go? I wanna go see the giraffes." She pronounced the word *jraffs,* running the syllables together.

"In a minute, sweetheart." Meeting Shelley's gaze again, he said, "I'll have Missy home about five. That okay with you?"

"Fine." She ducked down to look into the car. "Have fun, kids."

"We will!" they chorused.

Once they were gone, Shelley allowed herself to get angry. Oh, she couldn't stand John Taylor! Where did he get off thinking he was so great, anyway?

The way he'd acted this morning was the final straw. Here she'd tried to show him that she really did appreciate his help, that she didn't take it lightly or for granted, and what did he do? He threw her offer to reciprocate back in her face.

Well, Shelley had done her part. She'd offered to pay him back for today, and he'd refused. So, as far as she was concerned, that was the end of her obligation to him.

* * *

When they arrived at the zoo, and Patrick's dad, taking Nikki with him, went to buy their tickets, Missy and Patrick had a chance to talk.

"Things aren't going that great, are they?" Patrick said. "With your mom and my dad, I mean."

"Don't worry," Missy said. "When we get them together at Astroworld, it'll be fine, you'll see." Privately, she was a little bit worried herself, but she didn't want Patrick to know.

Patrick frowned. "I dunno. . . ."

"Oh, Patrick, don't be so *negative!*" Missy said, using the word her mother always used to describe people who were constantly casting doubt on everything. Missy's mom had told Missy over and over again that the worst thing a person could be was negative. Always look for the good things and not the bad, she'd told Missy when Missy got upset over something that happened or didn't happen.

"What does *negative* mean?" Patrick said.

Missy rolled her eyes. English and spelling were Patrick's two worst subjects. She had to explain the meanings of words to him all the time. Of course, he helped her with her math, so she guessed they were even. "It means you're thinking bad thoughts."

"Oh."

Just then Patrick's dad beckoned to them, so the two friends stopped talking and raced toward the entrance to the zoo. But just before Missy gave herself up to the excitement of the day ahead, she made herself a promise. She would do whatever she had to do to get her mom and Patrick's dad together. If the day at Astroworld didn't work, she'd find something else.

'Cause hadn't her mom always told her she could do anything she wanted to, if she wanted it badly enough? "Eventually, you'll reach your goal, Missy," she'd said over and over again. "If you just keep believing in yourself."

So we'll get them together, Missy told herself, *'cause I won't stop believing!*

John briefly wondered what Patrick and Missy were talking about that had them looking so serious, but he soon forgot about it in the flurry of getting them all through the turnstiles and then looking at the zoo map and deciding where they wanted to start.

"I wanna see the jraffs!" Nikki said.

"Oh, who wants to see the sorry old giraffes?" Patrick said. "I want to start with the lions!"

"Now, Patrick," John said, "the giraffes aren't sorry." He smiled down at Missy. "How about you, Missy? Do you have a preference?"

"No, Mr. Taylor. I don't care. I like all the animals," Missy said.

She was such an agreeable little kid, he thought. So sensible and wanting to please. The exact opposite of her mother. Well, he amended, maybe that assessment was unfair. Who knew? Maybe it was only he who brought out such disagreeable qualities in Shelley. Maybe around other people she was just as nice as Missy.

Thinking about Shelley, John remembered how she'd offered to take the kids out tomorrow and how he'd acted in the face of her offer. He was a little bit ashamed of himself. He could have been more pleasant, because the invitation really was a nice gesture on her part.

Why did Shelley always seem to rub him the wrong way, causing him to be abrupt and less than courteous? It wasn't his normal behavior. Among his family and friends he had always been known as "Mr. Nice Guy."

So why did he act like a complete jerk when he was with Shelley? Forget his manners and his upbringing and treat her in a manner bordering on rude?

He didn't know, but he didn't much like himself for doing it again today. He resolved that he would make amends when he saw her this evening. He might even say he'd been thinking about her offer to take the kids out and suggest another weekend.

His heart felt lighter after making this decision. "Tell you what," he said to the kids, "let's start with the birds. They're the closest. Then we can work our way up to the giraffes and elephants, come down through here..." he pointed at the map "...see the bears, then the cats, and finish up with the monkeys."

Chattering as excitedly as the birds they were headed toward, the kids skipped off ahead.

For the rest of the morning, they followed John's planned route, breaking twice—once to visit the rest rooms, and once to get a snack and something to drink.

After lunch, they resumed their leisurely foray through the remainder of the zoo. The kids were having a great time, and so was John. About three-thirty they had worked their way around to the monkey cages, and it was only then that John felt the creeping onset of the sadness that had been his silent companion for much of the past three years.

He swallowed hard, remembering.

Cathy had loved the monkeys. Whenever they had visited the zoo, she would send Patrick into fits of giggling by her mimicry of the monkeys' antics and sounds. Before he knew it, John would be laughing, too. And after Nikki was born, that last time they'd visited the zoo before Cathy's illness was diagnosed, even the baby had joined in their laughter.

John fought against the sadness. He didn't want to feel sad today. And he knew Cathy wouldn't want him to, either. Cathy had been an optimist, always seeing the bright side, just as she always focused on the best qualities of people instead of their faults.

Besides, the kids sensed when he was feeling sad, no matter how he tried to cover up. And he knew this awareness made them feel uncertain and vulnerable, even if they couldn't articulate their feelings.

Sometimes, like now, when he realized how much they depended on him, not only physically, but emotionally, John felt overwhelmed. The family's emotional well-being had always been Cathy's forte. She'd been the sensitive one, the one to draw out both him and the children, the one to say exactly the right thing and make everyone feel good about themselves. He'd always been the traditional provider of material things, the strong, silent one who would protect their home and family from harm.

Now he was expected to fill both roles.

He often felt overwhelmed . . . and scared. What if he couldn't? What if he wasn't? What if he let his children down? What if they needed something he wasn't giving them?

Stop it! Quit thinking that way. You're doing the best you can. That's all anyone can ask.

"Daddy? Daddy?"

John blinked. He looked down. Nikki was clutching a fistful of his blue jeans and shaking it to get his attention. He'd been so lost in his thoughts he hadn't noticed, and by the frustrated look on her face, Nikki had lost patience with him. "What, honey?"

"I gotta go to the baffroom," she said. "Bad."

Not for the first time, John was glad Missy was along. Otherwise, he would have had to take Nikki into the men's room, because there was no way he was going to let a five-year-old go alone into a public rest room. He and Patrick waited outside the ladies' rest room until the two little girls came out.

"I wash-ed my hands!" Nikki said, giving the word two syllables and making John smile.

"She used soap, too," Missy added.

"Well, now that we're all cleaned up, why don't we have some ice cream and then head on home?" John said.

He was rewarded with smiles and a happy chorus of agreement and by the time they'd reached the ice cream vendor, John had managed to put his doubts and fears behind him, at least for now.

Shelley was about to pull her hair out.

She had already shown Celia Van Doren twelve houses that day, and the woman hadn't liked any of them. There were only two more on Shelley's list of possibilities, and based on what Celia had objected to so far, Shelley wasn't very hopeful her client would like these next two any better than she'd liked the previous dozen.

"What are we looking at next?" Celia asked as she lowered the visor mirror and patted her frosted hair. She still looked every bit as cool and put-together as when the two women had started out.

"The next listing is an award-winning architectural design overlooking Buffalo Bayou," Shelley said, trying to keep her frustration from showing.

Celia returned the visor to its original position before turning to Shelley and giving her a raised-eyebrow look. "Contemporary, I'm assuming."

"Yes. But really lovely," Shelley rushed on. "Lots of windows."

Celia sighed. "It won't hurt to look at it, I suppose."

Shelley suppressed her own sigh. Scratch the contemporary, she thought, knowing it was going to be a waste of time to show it.

She was right.

Celia Van Doren obviously hated the house on sight.

She hated the next house, too. "And that's it?" she said, blue eyes narrowing.

Shelley didn't know what to do. She'd shown Celia everything listed in the area the woman had specified as the only part of Houston she'd consider. In desperation, Shelley decided to show Celia a listing the office staff at the agency had dubbed "Buckingham Palace" because it was so enormous and so ornate. "I've got one more I can show you right now. Otherwise, we'll have to go back to the office and run the listings again. Maybe I missed something." *Oh, great!*

Why did I say that? Now she'll think I'm incompetent!

But Celia Van Doren didn't comment, and Shelley hoped her blunder had passed unnoticed. As they drove to this last-gasp listing, Shelley thought furiously, trying to come up with something else, anything else, she might show Celia. Unfortunately, nothing else came to mind.

All too soon, they'd reached their destination.

"Oh, my..." Celia breathed as she climbed out of the car.

Shelley cringed inwardly as she looked at the architectural monstrosity before her. The house was owned by the heirs of a man who'd made millions in oil and spent a goodly portion of his money on all things gaudy, including huge baubles for his steady stream of blond, showgirl-type girlfriends and wives; six or seven obscenely expensive automobiles; and this ridiculously ostentatious dwelling. The house, a cross between Greek revival and Hollywood trash and flash, was three stories high and contained eight bedrooms and six bathrooms over its seven thousand plus square feet. Inside there was more gilt and marble and velvet and mirror than a person would find in Versailles.

"I adore it!" Celia Van Doren said before they'd even looked at half the house. "I absolutely adore it! How much do they want?"

Shelley could hardly breathe as she quoted the price. *This is crazy. Don't get your hopes up. She won't buy it. She's just curious, is all....*

"I want it," Celia announced. "Let's offer them..." She named a price somewhat below the asking price, but within a reasonable range.

Shelley felt almost light-headed as they drove back to her office so that Shelley could fill in a contract to take to the listing agent, who happened to be a co-worker. She wouldn't even let herself speculate on the outcome of the impending offer. She certainly wouldn't allow herself to calculate the amount of her commission should a sale go through. *Don't count your chickens,* she told herself. *Anything can happen. Remember Murphy's Law...*

Her hands were actually shaking when, barely two hours later, she handed the offer to Ginny Singer, the listing agent. And when Ginny, who hurriedly scanned the contract, gave Shelley a euphoric high five and said, ''Oh, God, Shelley, I can't *believe* this. I'll bet they take it! I'll call you as soon as I know anything!''

Shelley floated home. Or more accurately, her car seemed to float. She couldn't wait to tell someone, anyone, her good news, and yet she was afraid to count on it, despite Ginny's optimism.

When Shelley reached the house, she was greeted with a chorus of meows from her cats, who never failed to let her know they felt neglected when left alone all day long. ''If this sale goes through, it's catnip for everyone!'' Shelley promised, scratching their heads in order of their age—Daisy first, because she was fifteen and the elder stateswoman, then Romeo, and lastly, Juliette. Romeo and Juliette were littermates and seven years old.

After properly greeting her felines, Shelley headed for the phone. She told herself it wouldn't hurt to share her news with Linda Chapman, who, since Cathy's death, had become Shelley's closest friend and confidante. Linda was a librarian and worked at the branch library closest to Shelley, which was how the two women had met. They'd discovered a mutual love of theater and thrillers and now took a jazz dancing class together and talked on the phone nearly daily. Like Shelley, Linda was divorced, but she was childless. "Not by choice," she'd once confided. "Still, looking at how hard it is to raise a child alone, I sometimes think it all worked out for the best."

Linda was properly excited for Shelley when Shelley told her about Celia Van Doren and the offer.

"When will you know for sure?" she asked.

"Hopefully, tonight."

"I'll keep my fingers crossed."

"Thanks. Say a prayer or two, too, will you?"

"Of course."

They talked about other things for a while, then Linda said, "How'd Mr. Cold Fish act today when he picked up Missy?"

"Actually, he started out being pretty nice," Shelley said, going on to explain how John had ended by making her mad once again. "I don't know why. I try not to get mad at him, but I can't seem to help it. He just rubs me the wrong way. The only time we've ever spent any time at all together without me getting irritated about something he said or did was when Cathy was sick. Of course, then all he cared about was making Cathy as happy as possible, so he worked hard to be nice to me."

"Hey, I don't blame you for feeling the way you do. I'd feel exactly the same way, too. After all, he's made it plain he doesn't like you. You know what I think.

He was jealous of your relationship with his wife, and he still resents you.''

Shelley frowned. "He had no reason to be jealous. Cathy adored him. I was certainly no threat to him or his marriage. Besides, even though I thought Cathy needed to assert herself more, I certainly would never have tried to cause trouble between them.''

"Oh, go figure," Linda said. "Who can understand the male species? Who even wants to? Quit worrying about it. You did the right thing today. You offered to pay him back, he refused, your obligation is now over.''

Shelley laughed. "Thanks, old buddy. You're right. I'm not going to worry about it. I'm too happy to worry about anything!''

"So hey, if the sale goes through—which it's going to, I'm absolutely positive—do you want to celebrate? Maybe spring for tickets for that new Tommy Tune show opening at Jones Hall next month? We can get all gussied up, have dinner somewhere really nice, like Brennan's, then go to the show. What do you say?''

"It's a date.''

After they hung up, Shelley couldn't seem to settle down. She was too hyped. Too nervous. God, she hoped she didn't have to wait long before getting an answer from Ginny. When the phone rang a scant fifteen minutes later, she couldn't believe it when she heard Ginny's voice. So soon! For the second time that day, Shelley held her breath. "They were home, they read the offer, and they accepted it on the spot!'' Ginny said. "They didn't even counter-offer. Can you *believe* it? I'm so thrilled, Shelley, I could just kiss you!''

Shelley replaced the receiver in a daze. And she finally allowed herself to think about her commission. Although her portion, as the selling agent, was only one quarter of the entire commission, it was still more than she had ever made in an entire year working at the secretarial job she'd had before she married and twice as much as she'd made the previous year working as a checker at the local supermarket while she worked toward her real estate license.

This commission would mean she could put aside something toward a down payment on a house of their own, plus she would be able to give Missy those gymnastics lessons she so wanted as well as have enough to live on for many months.

She was so happy she danced around the kitchen. What a wonderful day this had turned out to be!

When John and the children arrived at the house barely half an hour later, her jubilation had reached fever pitch, and she even felt magnanimous toward John.

After the kids had excitedly related all the high points of the day, with John smiling indulgently throughout, Shelley said, "Well, I've had a wonderful day, too! I sold a big house, and I'm in the mood to celebrate. What say we all go out for pizza? My treat?"

"Goody, goody, pizza!" Nikki said.

"Can we go, Dad, huh? Can we?" Patrick said.

"Well..." John said. He looked down at his kids.

Missy smiled hopefully, her gaze traveling from Shelley to John and back to Shelley again.

Shelley waited. She wondered how John planned to get out of this. She also wondered why she'd put herself in this position again.

John's gaze slowly rose to meet hers. Shelley geared herself to accept his refusal graciously.

And then he smiled with real warmth. "Sounds like fun. We accept."

For the second time that day, Shelley was stunned. But she recovered quickly. "Good. Just let me get my purse, and we can be on our way." She wondered if it was the pressure from the kids that had made John accept or whether, for the first time, he was actually warming up. Then she decided his reasons didn't matter. He was coming. The kids were coming. And Shelley was determined that they would all have a good time.

No matter what.

Chapter Three

"Circus Time, we wanna go to Circus Time!" Missy and Patrick said.

"Yeah, Circus Time," Nikki parroted.

Shelley grinned. "Circus Time it is."

She'd taken Missy there many times. The restaurant featured all kinds of video games for kids to play, and a clown strolled between the tables and booths and entertained the diners. In keeping with the circus motif, the waiters and waitresses wore the outfits of circus performers.

Somehow Shelley found herself sitting next to John in one of the booths lining the outer walls of the huge establishment. She wasn't quite sure how it happened.

The seating was awkward, she felt, because it was easier to talk to someone who was sitting across the table from you than to turn your head and converse with someone next to you. Plus there was something too intimate about sitting so close in a booth, and she felt uncomfortable.

Once again, the thought crossed her mind that the kids were trying to matchmake. This time, instead of dismissing the notion as absurd, Shelley seriously considered it. The idea amused her. Why the kids would try to get her and John together, she couldn't imagine. She almost felt sorry for them, because their scheme, if that's what it was, was doomed to failure.

After the lion-tamer waiter took their order and brought their drinks, all three kids wanted to play video games.

"Why not wait until after we eat?" John suggested.

"Oh, *Dad*..." Patrick said. "We wanna go now."

"Mom..." Missy said.

Nikki just looked at them big-eyed.

Laughing, knowing when they were beaten, Shelley and John dug out their loose change.

"Now you'll keep an eye on Nikki, won't you?" John said to Patrick. "She's not old enough to play the games by herself."

"I know."

"Don't worry, Mr. Taylor," Missy piped in. "She'll be okay. I'll watch her."

Shelley smiled proudly as Missy, carefully holding Nikki's hand, walked off with Patrick.

"That's a really nice kid you've got," John said.

"Thank you. I think she's wonderful. In fact, I don't know what I'd do without her."

"She's very grown-up for her age."

"Yes." What was he saying? That Shelley had forced Missy to grow up too soon? *Oh, quit reading something critical into his every word. Give the guy a chance.* "Sometimes I worry about that."

"About what? That she's maturing too fast?"

"No, not exactly."

John turned slightly to face her. She wished there were more room on the leather seat. He was too close. It made her feel funny.

"Well, what then?" he said. Before she could answer, he added, "I'm going to move to the other side of the booth. It's too hard to talk this way."

Shelley immediately felt more relaxed once he'd settled across from her. "What worries me is maybe she's *too* independent."

"I don't think you need to worry."

"You don't?"

"Nope. She seems pretty levelheaded to me."

"But..." *Oh, go ahead, say it.* "Sometimes I feel bad. I think maybe she's been cheated. Forced to grow up too quickly and take on too many responsibilities."

He nodded thoughtfully. "Because of the divorce."

"Yes."

"Well, I can understand why that might concern you. My kids have had to deal with losing their mother, and even though they seem to be doing well, I still worry about them and how it's all affected them."

His eyes had clouded at the mention of Cathy, and Shelley could see that even though nearly three years had passed, her death was still difficult for him. "I guess parents just worry about their kids, period," she said.

He grimaced. "And no wonder. Parenting is a scary job. What if you let them down and they're scarred for life? Sometimes I feel completely overwhelmed by the responsibility."

"Really? I never would have guessed you felt that way."

He frowned. "Why do you say that?"

"Oh, I don't know...you've always seemed so sure of yourself. I never imagined *you* to have any self-doubts." She hadn't really meant to emphasize the word "you"—it just seemed to come out that way.

His gaze clung to hers for a long moment. "In other words, you think of me as a self-righteous jerk."

Shelley flushed. "I didn't say that."

His mouth twisted in a wry smile. "You didn't have to."

Damn! Why was it she was always putting her foot in her mouth with him? And he was trying so hard to be nice tonight.... "John, I'm sorry, I really didn't—"

"Look, it's okay. I guess I *have* acted pretty smug and know-it-all around you, haven't I?"

"But I didn't mean what I said to sound that way. It's just that I was surprised by your admission. And...well, I guess I always think I'm the only person who's got self-doubts." She gave an embarrassed little laugh. "You know—everyone else is sure of themselves and knows exactly what to do...."

He started to reply then stopped as their waiter approached with their pizza. After the waiter had served the food and left, John said, "I'll go get the kids."

For the next half hour, the five of them ate their pizza and drank their drinks and the talk remained general and casual. But then the kids took off again, and Shelley once more found herself alone with John.

"So tell me about that sale you made today," he said. Shelley, relieved not to go back to the more sensitive subject they'd explored earlier, launched into a description of the day.

"To appreciate this, you've got to be able to picture my client. Celia Van Doren is one of those women who doesn't sweat—you know the type—perfectly put-together at all times. Makeup always impeccable, hair never out of place, and when she wears linen, she never looks wrinkled." She grinned. "She also keeps her nose canted at a forty-five degree angle." Shelley lifted her face to demonstrate. She'd always had the gift of being able to capture voices and mannerisms, so her depiction of Celia Van Doren was pretty much on target.

By the time she finished describing Celia's reactions throughout the day, John was laughing without restraint. "I'd never have the patience to deal with someone like that."

"Oh, sure you would, if your livelihood depended on it." Once again, Shelley was reminded of how different their circumstances were. John worked in a family business, and he did not deal directly with the customers, either.

"So how old a woman is this Mrs. Van Doren?" he said.

"Oh, I don't know. Early fifties, maybe. Obviously loaded, because that monstrosity she bought was listed for two million."

He whistled. "Two million... imagine having that kind of money. How'd you happen to get her?"

"Totally by chance. She called about one of our listings and I was the only agent in the office at the time, so the receptionist passed the call on to me." Shelley drew circles in the condensation on her root beer mug. "It was really such a fluke, because it turns out Mrs. Van Doren was already working with another, very prestigious agency, but her particular agent happened to be out of town, and she saw our listing, and she ended up switching and working with me." Shelley's smile was wry. "That other agent probably hates my guts."

"I'll bet. And wait'll they find out you sold her a two million dollar house."

"I know. Boy, you should see the house. It's tacky. The taste-police would probably condemn it."

He chuckled. "As long as the client likes it, who cares?"

"My sentiments exactly."

"Do you like selling real estate?"

"Yes. Funny thing is, I picked the field because I felt it was something I could do where I might have a chance to make a decent living and not because I had a burning desire to do it. The other thing was, the training time was so much less than a four-year college program for other fields. It was a gamble, but it worked out, because now I find I not only like it but I seem to have an aptitude for it."

"That's great. Nothing more important than enjoying what you do for a living and doing it well."

Shelley nodded. "I know. The only bad part—as you know—is the erratic hours. I hate having to be away from Missy in the evenings or on the weekends and really try not to schedule appointments for those times unless it's absolutely necessary." She waited for him to make a derogatory remark, but he didn't. His expression remained friendly and understanding, and the last vestiges of Shelley's negative feelings toward him vanished.

For the first time since she'd known him, she could see exactly what it was Cathy had loved about him. For one thing, he was a darned good listener. Shelley appreciated a good listener. Too many men she'd known loved to hear themselves talk, but were terrible at listening to anyone else, especially women.

Her ex was a prime example. Barry could discourse for hours on his thoughts and his experiences, but he had a glazed look in his eyes after listening to Shelley for more than ten minutes at a stretch. Of course, Barry was totally self-involved, convinced he was the most interesting person in any gathering.

John also had a good sense of humor, an absolutely essential quality in a man, as far as Shelley was concerned. And lastly, he was a wonderful father. She'd always known that. It was obvious he doted on his children, and it was just as obvious they returned his love.

Shelley couldn't help comparing his relationship with his children to Barry's with Missy. Barry, who had wanted a son. Barry, who acted as if Missy didn't exist. No wonder Missy loved John!

John wondered what Shelley was thinking as silence fell between them. It wasn't an uncomfortable silence, but it was obvious that something had caused her to become pensive.

Finally, she sighed softly and smiled at him. "You know what?"

"What?"

"You're a very nice guy."

Why was it he'd never noticed what a really pretty smile she had? He grinned. "You sound surprised."

She laughed. "Maybe I am. But it's a nice surprise."

Her gray eyes, which he'd always thought were so cold-looking, twinkled with merriment. Her skin was slightly flushed, and a few strands of her fine, blond hair had escaped its careful styling. Dressed as she was in denim shorts, a navy T-shirt and navy sneakers, she looked younger and more appealing than she'd ever looked before. Or maybe he'd just never realized she *could* look this way. More accurately, maybe this was the first time he'd given her a chance to show this side of herself. He was a bit astonished to find he was attracted to her. The knowledge brought excitement, followed quickly by a surge of guilt.

How could he possibly be attracted to Shelley? She was nothing like Cathy. Nothing at all.

For the rest of the evening, he struggled with his new awareness. It cast a pall over his enjoyment of the evening, and he felt a mixture of relief and regret when Shelley finally said, "We'd better go, don't you think? It's nearly eight o'clock."

The kids were rambunctious and giggled and chattered all the way home, so John was spared the necessity of making conversation. Unfortunately, he could still think and he was very aware of Shelley sitting next to him in the front seat of the car. He kept sneaking glances her way, unable to keep his gaze from the sight of her shapely legs and thighs or the elegant line of her throat or the round curve of her breasts.

He told himself the only reason she held such sudden fascination for him was his long spell without a woman. *It's hormones, pure and simple.*

Finally they reached their street. John pulled his car into Shelley's driveway and let the motor idle. "Thanks for dinner," he said. "It was fun, wasn't it, kids?" He avoided Shelley's eyes, afraid he'd give away his thoughts.

"Yeah," chorused Patrick and Nikki.

"And thank *you* for taking Missy with you today," Shelley said.

"My pleasure." He finally met her gaze.

"Well, good night," she said.

"Good night."

Missy climbed out of the back seat and mother and daughter walked across the lawn to the front door. John backed out of the driveway and pulled into his own across the street. When he and the kids went into the house, Froggie was home and sitting in the kitchen drinking a cup of tea. She looked at the clock. "I thought you'd be home hours ago."

John started guiltily. He'd forgotten to call Froggie! She'd probably been worried. "I'm sorry, Froggie. I should have called you. We, uh, went out for pizza with Shelley and Missy."

Froggie gave him an odd little smile. "Oh, really? That's nice."

Nikki climbed up on Froggie's lap and snuggled her head under Froggie's chin. "I like Missy."

Froggie smiled down at her. "I know you do."

"Her mom's nice, too," Patrick said.

"Yes, she is," Froggie agreed, her blue-eyed gaze meeting John's. The odd look was still there.

"Shelley made a big sale today, so she offered to take us all out. Also, I think she was grateful we took Missy to the zoo." Now why had he felt the need to explain? He could have kicked himself. He should have just let her remark pass without comment. For a while now, she'd been hinting that it was time for him to think about dating again, and if she got the idea he was at all interested in Shelley, the next thing he knew, she'd be matchmaking.

"So did you have fun?" Froggie asked.

The kids both started telling her about the day, giving John a chance to collect himself, and when they'd finished, Froggie suggested it was time for Nikki's bath, and Patrick went to his room, enabling John to escape to the family room where he switched on the TV. But no matter how he tried, he couldn't concentrate on the program.

His thoughts continued to veer to the woman in the house across the street. Even if he were ready for a new relationship—which he wasn't—Shelley was all wrong for him. When and if he ever married again, he wanted a woman like Cathy. Someone who would be happy to stay at home and be a wife and mother. Someone who had no aspirations toward a career of her own. And someone who did not come with all kinds of problems and baggage. He had enough to contend with. He didn't need any more.

He locked up and climbed the stairs. By the time he'd readied himself for bed, he'd decided the best course of action would be to relegate Shelley to her old place in his life. She was Missy's mother and his

across-the-street neighbor. Nothing more. Yes. That's
the way he would think of her from now on.

Shelley had a hard time falling asleep. She was too
exhilarated from her day. The sale, the relaxed evening with John, her discovery that she actually liked
him, all combined to keep her awake and thinking.

Several times she got up and walked to her window, which faced the street. There was a big full moon
lighting the neighborhood, casting a silvery glow over
everything. A breeze stirred the leaves on the mostly
mature trees lining their block. The next-door neighbor's dog barked. Somewhere in the distance a police
siren wailed. Farther down the street came the sound
of a car's ignition. Normal sights and sounds, all of
them.

Most of the houses on her street were dark. Although it was a Saturday night, Shelley's neighbors
were mostly families who kept early hours.

She looked at John's house. A pale light shone from
the kitchen window on the driveway side. Shelley knew
it was probably the light over the stove. Cathy said
once that John was in the habit of waking up in the
middle of the night and going downstairs for a glass of
milk.

"I don't want him to break his neck," she'd said,
smiling. "I like his neck too much. So I keep a light on
in the kitchen and a night-light in the hallway."

At the time, Shelley had been made wistful by the
look of love on Cathy's face. To cover the ache of
loneliness that crept over her, she said, "Doesn't he
wake you when he gets up? I'd hate that."

"I don't mind." She gazed at Shelley through her lashes. Her smile turned secretive.

All at once Shelley knew the reason Cathy didn't mind John's nocturnal prowling was that when John came back to their bed, they made love. She wasn't sure how she knew; the knowledge was just there.

Remembering that conversation now, the same emotions she'd felt then returned. She closed her eyes. It had been so long since she'd shared a bed with a man, and even when she had—especially the last couple of years—she'd never felt that closeness and sense of true intimacy that Cathy and John seemed to have felt. Barry had always made Shelley feel as if she wasn't measuring up to his expectations. There'd been no real give and take between them, no sense of sharing—simply Barry's demands and Shelley's efforts to please.

Shelley opened her eyes again and looked at the dark second-floor windows of John's house. She couldn't see his bedroom window. It faced the back yard. She wondered if he ever lay awake nights. *Of course, he does. He still misses Cathy. You could see it written all over his face tonight.* Shelley wondered what it must be like for him in terms of the loss of their physical relationship.

It must be hell.

Shelley wondered if it might not be better, after all, to have never had what John and Cathy had had, because at least then you didn't really know what you were missing. You could imagine, as she did, but you didn't *know.* Even as the thought formed, she rejected it.

Even if I knew I was going to lose it, I'd still rather have had what they had than never experience it at all.

Maybe someday, she told herself as she climbed back into bed. Maybe someday she would meet some wonderful man who would think she was equally wonderful, and . . .

The thought trailed off.

But not anytime soon. I'm not ready. First I have to make sure Missy's and my future is secure.

She laughed at herself. What was she getting all melancholy about, anyway? She was happy with her life and her independence.

Telling herself it must have been the full moon causing her to get goofy, she punched up her pillow, closed her eyes, and went to sleep.

The following morning, John and the kids had just gotten home from church and were changing their clothes in preparation for going to his mother's home for dinner, when the front doorbell rang.

"I'll get it!" Patrick called.

A few minutes later, Patrick poked his head around the doorway to John's bedroom. "Dad?"

John, who'd finished dressing and was now in his bathroom brushing his teeth, said, "Yes? Who is it, Patrick?"

"It's Missy. She has something she wants to ask you."

"Okay. Be there in a minute." John finished brushing his teeth, then walked into the bedroom. Missy and Patrick were both standing just inside the doorway.

"Hi, Mr. Taylor," Missy said. She was dressed in a pretty green-striped dress and had a matching bow in her hair.

"Hi, Missy. You look pretty today."

She smiled shyly. "Thanks. I just got home from Sunday school."

"We just got home from church, too," Patrick said.

"Well, what can I do for you today?" John said.

"Uh, you know Thursday's my birthday...."

"Yes, Patrick told me."

"And my mom said I could ask two friends to go to Astroworld with me on Saturday...."

John smiled. "And you want to know if it's okay for Patrick to go?"

"Well..." She fidgeted a little. "Yes, but I, uh, wanted to invite you to go, too," she finished in a rush.

John blinked. "Me?"

She shook her head vigorously. "Uh-huh."

"You're inviting *me* instead of another school friend?"

"Uh-huh." She ducked her head.

Had Shelley put Missy up to inviting him? Maybe she couldn't chaperon the party and he was a convenient substitute. He hated the negative thought, but what other reason could there be for Missy to invite him to join her party? "It's very nice of you to ask me," he said warily. "Uh, is your mother going?"

"Oh, yes," Missy said. "She's going."

John was a bit ashamed of himself for his suspicions, but after some of the things that had happened lately, no one would really blame him for thinking what he had.

"I really want you to come, Mr. Taylor. Will you?" Missy said.

John couldn't help feeling touched by the invitation, even though he still couldn't imagine why she wanted him in preference to someone her own age. "I'm flattered to be asked, and yes, if you really want me, I'll come."

She gave Patrick a quick, almost triumphant glance, then turned back to John with a happy smile on her face and an excited gleam in her eyes. "Gee, thanks, Mr. Taylor. It's gonna be so much fun!"

After Missy left to go back home, and Patrick went downstairs, John thought about that look that had passed between them. There was something odd about it. Hell, there was something odd about her invitation! What were the kids up to?

Well, knowing kids, John was sure he would find out sooner or later. But in the meantime, he'd see if he couldn't get Patrick to tell him by some judicious questioning.

Shelley had been doing some hand laundry when Missy asked if she could go over to Patrick's for a few minutes because she'd forgotten to ask him about Astroworld.

After Missy left, Shelley finished her washing and thought about cleaning house, then decided she had better things to do with a beautiful Sunday afternoon than spend it doing housework. Maybe she and Missy would go shopping. There'd been so little money in the past year to buy anything new for either one of them, and what money they did have, Shelley had had to invest in her professional wardrobe. She'd felt guilty about spending the money on herself, but looking successful was very important when you were a real estate agent. It told your clients they could have confidence in you, that you were doing well, which equated with knowing your business.

Still, as a mother, she wanted to do things for Missy. And now, thanks to Celia Van Doren's unfathomable taste in houses, Shelley could afford to indulge Missy just a little.

And she would.

What the heck. They'd make a day of it. Go out to West Oaks Mall, shop a bit, maybe even see a movie if there was anything suitable for a kid to see, and then top off the day with dinner at Taco Cabana, one of their favorite places.

She briefly thought that she'd be in big trouble if anything happened and her deal fell through before closing, but hastily rid herself of the thought. Nothing would happen. *Don't be negative.*

She was smiling and ready to go when Missy returned to the house about ten minutes later. "So what did Patrick say?"

"He's gonna go." Missy smiled.

"Good. Who else are you going to ask?"

"Well, uh..." Missy evaded her eyes. "I dunno yet," she mumbled.

Missy's entire body language told Shelley she wasn't telling the truth. What was going on? "Come on, Missy, you're not a very good liar," Shelley prodded gently.

Missy shuffled her feet.

"Missy..."

"I asked Mr. Taylor."

"You asked Mr. Taylor if Patrick could go."

"No, I, uh..." Missy finally looked up. Her gray-eyed gaze met Shelley's. "I asked Mr. Taylor to go, too."

Shelley's mouth fell open. "What? Why?"

"'Cause I wanted him to go. 'Cause I *like* him."

Shelley stared at her daughter. It was on the tip of her tongue to say no, yet how could she? What reason would she give? *I don't want to spend an entire day with John Taylor, Missy, because I don't want to become attracted to him....* Oh, sure! *Think!* "Missy," she said slowly, "you know, maybe Mr. Taylor doesn't want to go to Astroworld."

"He said yes!"

"Well, maybe he didn't want to hurt your feelings."

"No, Mom," Missy said emphatically, "he wants to go. He even asked if *you* were going, then he said he was *flattered* to be asked."

Shelley knew when she was beaten. There was no help for it. John was accompanying them to Astroworld, whether Shelley liked it or not.

Chapter Four

Shelley set her alarm for five o'clock Thursday morning so that she could bake Missy's birthday cake before leaving for work. By the time Missy came downstairs at seven, the three-layer chocolate cake was cooling on wire racks and Shelley had made the frosting.

She'd also fixed a special breakfast of pancakes and link sausages, and Missy's gifts and a card were stacked neatly next to her plate.

Just then Missy walked into the kitchen.

"Happy birthday, Melissa Ann Broome!" Shelley walked over to give Missy a hug and kiss.

Missy smiled happily.

After they ate their breakfast, Shelley said, "Okay, toots, time to open your presents."

Eyes shining, Missy reached for the card first.

"Why don't you save that for last?" Shelley suggested.

"Okay." She unwrapped a small, oblong box and squealed with delight when she discovered a Barbie watch. "Oh, Mom, I love it! Thank you." The watch was promptly strapped around Missy's wrist. Next came a larger, flat box which revealed purple leotards and tights and black ballet slippers. Missy's eyes got wide.

Shelley smiled around the lump in her throat.

When Missy opened the card, which not only wished her a very happy birthday but informed her that she was signed up for gymnastics lessons starting the following week, the look on her face caused the lump to get even bigger.

"Oh, Mom..." she breathed, hurling herself off her chair and into Shelley's arms. "Oh, thank you, thank you. It's just what I wanted!"

"You're very welcome, sweetie."

After Missy ran off to catch the school bus down at the corner, Shelley cleaned up the kitchen, frosted and decorated the birthday cake, then put it in the refrigerator where the cats couldn't bother with it. As she worked, she thought about how wonderful it was to be able to make your child happy. Especially when that child was so deserving of being happy.

For the rest of the day, on and off between talking to clients and even while showing a prospective buyer several town homes, one of which he seemed really interested in, Shelley kept remembering Missy's happiness that morning. But underneath the feeling of satisfaction was a niggling worry. Although Missy hadn't mentioned anything about her father that morning, Shelley knew she would be eagerly looking for a phone call and card when she got home from school.

Please, God, don't let Barry disappoint her....

Shelley called home at three to see if Mrs. Dunbar was there. "Has the mail come yet?" Shelley asked the older woman.

"Yes, ma'am. I brought it in a few minutes ago."

"Did Missy get a card from Colorado?"

"Just a minute. I'll check."

Shelley held her breath until the sitter came back to the phone. "Yes, ma'am, she sure did."

"Just one?"

"Yes, ma'am."

"What's the return address?"

"It's 7980 Goldenrod."

Shelley's heart sank. Her parents. Although she was glad they'd remembered—as they sometimes didn't—if she'd had to choose, she would have preferred Barry to have been the sender.

Well, he might still come through. Maybe a gift would arrive by UPS later that afternoon or maybe he'd call and say something was on the way but would be late. Once again, she breathed a silent prayer.

But when Shelley arrived home at six, there had been no delivery and no phone call. She didn't have to ask. Missy's silence on the subject told her everything she needed to know.

Shelley gritted her teeth. If Barry let Missy down again... *Don't be negative. He'll call her later.*

By seven, they'd finished their dinner of broiled chicken breasts, rice and salad, and Shelley brought out the birthday cake. Romeo, the most curious of their cats, promptly jumped up on the table to get a closer look. Laughing, Shelley shooed him away and he stalked off, meowing his indignation.

Shelley lit the eight candles. "Okay, make a wish, sweetie."

Missy closed her eyes briefly, then opened them and blew out her candles.

At eight, Shelley's sister called. Suzanne and Shelley were not close, partly because Suzanne rarely thought about anyone except herself—which wasn't surprising since their mother had always acted as if Suzanne was the center of the universe. Yet Suzanne did seem to have a soft spot for Missy.

"How are you doing?" Suzanne said when she'd finished talking to Missy.

"Great," Shelley said. "I just sold a big house."

"That's nice."

Shelley smiled wryly. She could hear the lack of interest in her sister's voice. "How about you? What's new in your life?"

Suzanne needed no other encouragement to launch into an impassioned description of the "wonderful" new man she'd met. "And we flew to Sun Valley in his private jet," she finished a full ten minutes later. "It was fabulous. I saw Brad Pitt and Julia Roberts and Sly Stallone with that model he's seeing now—I can't think of her name—but she's gorgeous."

"Imagine that."

"We stayed in this fantastic condo that Gary owns. He also owns a penthouse apartment in Manhattan and a fabulous house in Beverly Hills and a beach house on Longboat Key in Florida," Suzanne gushed on.

"Wow," Shelley said, forcing enthusiasm into her voice and wondering if Suzanne had any inkling of how impossible it was for Shelley to relate to this kind of life-style.

"And I *think* he's going to give me a ring for Christmas."

"That's great." Shelley tried to remember if this would be Suzanne's fifth or sixth engagement. If this Gary person actually married her, it would be her third marriage.

"Well . . ." Suzanne's voice trailed off.

"Well . . ."

After a short, awkward silence, Suzanne laughed and said, "Gotta run. Tell Missy her birthday check is in the mail."

"I'll do that. Thanks for calling."

After hanging up, Shelley said, "Aunt Suzanne said she's mailed you a check."

"Yeah," Missy said. "She told me. And Grandma said in her card that she and Grandpa sent me something and it'll probably come tomorrow."

What about you, Barry?

As the clock crept around to nine-thirty, Missy's normal bedtime, the phone remained ominously silent. Shelley wondered what Missy was thinking but hated to bring up the subject. Maybe she should, though. Oh, God, she could just *kill* Barry. How could he do this to Missy?

She was still debating whether or not to say anything to Missy when she went into her room to kiss her good-night.

"'Night, sweetie," she said, brushing her lips against Missy's cheek. "Sleep tight." Her eyes met Missy's.

"Mom? You know what I wished? When I blew out my candles?"

The look in Missy's eyes caused the lump to return, bigger than ever. Shelley's heart actually hurt as she looked down into her daughter's eyes. Their soft gray depths were filled with an ineffable sadness.

"I wished Dad would call me tonight," Missy whispered, "but he didn't."

In that moment, Shelley was glad that Barry lived so far away, because if he'd been anywhere close, Shelley might have driven to his house and done something she'd be sorry for later—like murder him. How *could* he do this to Missy?

She silently vowed that she would never, ever, let Missy down. And she would do everything in her power to make up to her daughter for her father's neglect.

It was a struggle to keep her rage hidden. "He'll probably call tomorrow, or maybe even over the weekend," she said gently. "I'll bet he's out of town. You know how much he has to travel for his job."

Missy nodded. "Maybe."

"I'm sure that's it." Shelley bent over and kissed Missy again, holding her close for a long moment. "I love you so much, sweetie. You're the best daughter in the entire world."

"I love you, too, Mom." Missy's voice was steady, but the look of sadness remained in her eyes.

Shelley knew she'd never forget that look. Nor would she forget who had put it there.

* * *

Saturday dawned clear and bright. The weatherman said the temperature would climb to the high eighties but the humidity would remain low.

A perfect day, Shelley thought as she and Missy waited for John and Patrick to arrive.

Missy looked at the clock. It was two minutes after nine. "I told them we wanted to leave at nine. Where are they?"

Shelley chuckled. "Don't be so impatient, sweetie. They'll be here."

The words were no sooner out of Shelley's mouth when the doorbell rang and Missy, grinning, raced off to answer it.

Shelley blew kisses to the cats, picked up the tote she'd filled earlier and headed toward the front door.

"I'll bet you were surprised to find out Missy'd invited me to go today," John said in greeting. His accompanying smile was warm and friendly.

Shelley felt a little thrill of excitement as their eyes met. She thought he looked great in his navy shorts, white knit shirt and Astros baseball cap. Funny how, in all the years she'd known him, she'd never before noticed what nice-looking legs he had—actually, just how all-around sexy he was. "Well, yes," she said, smiling back, "it was a little unexpected."

There was an approving gleam in his eyes as his gaze swept her. She was suddenly glad she'd worn her new red shorts with the matching red and white striped T-shirt. After all, even though she wasn't ready for a relationship, it was nice to know that an attractive man found you attractive, too.

"Come on, Mom," Missy said, heading toward the car. "Let's go."

"We're coming," Shelley said. She looked at John again. "I hope you don't mind if we stop by my office on the way. I have to drop off some papers. It'll only take a few minutes extra."

"Tell you what," he said. "Why don't I just drive, too, and we'll meet you there."

"Oh, there's no reason for you to have to do that."

"Well, I know, but actually it might save me some time later. After we come home today, I was going to have to drive over to my brother's house, because he's got some contracts I need, and he's going out of town tomorrow. But if I've got my own car, I can just stop by there on the way home."

"If you're sure..."

"I'm sure."

"Okay, then, we'll meet you at the entrance."

"But, Mom," Missy protested. "I wanted to ride there with Patrick."

"You can still ride with him," John said. "Unless your mother minds."

"I don't mind." Shelley couldn't help thinking how different John's attitude was than it had been in the recent past.

"Okay. See you soon," John said.

The kids were practically jumping up and down with excitement when they all met at the entrance to the park about an hour later. Shelley bought the tickets and handed them out, smiling at John as the kids raced off to go through the turnstiles ahead of them.

"They're certainly wound up," John said. "They never stopped talking all the way here."

"We'll probably be exhausted by the end of the day."

"I don't know about you, but I intend to spend a lot of time sitting on benches just watching." His eyes twinkled. "I don't want Patrick to know it, but some of these rides scare the liver out of me."

She laughed. "Chicken."

"And proud of it," he said.

"We wanna ride XLR8 first," Patrick said, naming the kids' favorite roller coaster.

"Why am I not surprised?" John said.

He and Shelley exchanged an amused look and the four of them headed toward the ride.

When the kids realized Shelley and John weren't intending to ride with them, they objected loudly. Finally, laughing, John said, "Okay, okay, you win. I'll ride. How about you, Shelley?"

"Guess I have no choice."

For the next couple of hours, the four of them rode every roller coaster in the park that allowed kids the size of Missy and Patrick. Sometimes all four of them sat together, and sometimes John sat with Patrick and Shelley sat with Missy. Once the kids sat together and John and Shelley sat in the seat behind them, and during the ride John put his arm around Shelley. It felt so nice, Shelley hated for the ride to end.

They also rode things like Warp 2,000 and the Six-Shooter and The Bamboo Shoot. At the climax of the The Bamboo Shoot, as their boat swooshed down the hill of water, they got their picture taken. It cost eight dollars for a print, and John insisted on buying two—one for Patrick and one for Missy.

After lunch Shelley suggested they head for the antique cars. "That way we can sit and just let our food digest," she told John.

"Thank God."

She laughed.

John and Shelley headed for a bench in the shade which would give them a good vantage point, and Missy and Patrick entered the queue for the cars.

Shelley sank down gratefully. It was good to get out of the sun. Although the September day wasn't as hot as some they'd had lately, the sun was still pretty strong. She could feel its effects on her nose and realized that even though she was wearing sunscreen, she should have also worn a hat like John.

"It feels good to sit," she said.

"Yes," John agreed. He leaned back on the bench, his legs stretched out in front of him.

"Is Froggie watching Nikki today?"

"No. I took her over to my brother Mark's house last night, and she's spending the day there."

"Now which one is Mark?"

He turned and gave her a quizzical smile. "You sound as if you know about my brothers."

"Well, Cathy talked about your family a lot."

He nodded. "She liked my family."

"Yes, she did. She made them sound like the ideal American family."

"They are pretty nice people."

Shelley felt a stab of envy. From the warmth in John's voice and the smile that still hovered around his mouth, she knew there was a lot of love in his feelings toward his brothers and sister. She thought of her parents, how remote they were most of the time—not only in terms of distance but in terms of an emotional connection—and her sister, whom Shelley rarely saw and only talked with every few months.

"You asked about Mark," John said. "He's the second oldest. Let's see, he'll be thirty-eight in December."

"Tell me about all of them."

"Oh, come on, you don't have to be polite."

"No, I really want to know."

"Okay, you asked for it. First comes Luke, he's forty, almost forty-one, I guess. He's a photographer, and he and his wife, Clem, who's a journalist with WNN, travel all over the world. They just recently had twins. Then comes Mark. He's married to Clem's sister, Miranda, and they just had their first baby. After him comes Matthew, he's thirty-five. He's still single."

"And what do Mark and Matthew do?"

"They both work for our company. They're field agents."

"Field agents. You mean they provide security to your clients?"

"Yep. I used to do that, too, but after Cathy died, I felt it was important to get away from the traveling and sometimes danger of the work, so I took over as the number cruncher."

Shelley realized anew how many changes Cathy's death had made in John's life. "Did you mind?"

"Uh-uh. I never liked field work that much."

"So after you comes who?"

"Paul. He's twenty-nine. He also works for the company, and he and his wife, Molly, have two kids.

Then comes James. He's twenty-six and a resident at Jones Hospital.''

"And you have a sister, too, right?"

John smiled. "Yeah. Rebecca. She's everyone's favorite. She's thirty-two, almost thirty-three, a year younger than me. She lives in Cleveland.''

"Texas?"

"No, Ohio.''

"What does she do?"

"Works for an advertising agency.''

"And your father is dead. . . .''

John nodded. "Yeah. I was thirteen when he died, and I still miss him.''

Shelley couldn't even imagine a family like John had described. All those brothers and a sister. And obviously all close. Plus their spouses and the nieces and nephews. It sounded too good to be true. Almost like living in "The Donna Reed Show" where everyone smiled and loved each other and no one argued or was jealous or mean. And on top of all that, John had Cathy's Aunt Froggie. How did one person get so lucky? "I've always wondered what it would be like to have a family like yours,'' she said pensively.

John shrugged. "We're nothing special.''

"Oh, but you are.''

"You only think so because we're big. . . .''

"No, it's more than that. You're close. You care about each other. I can hear it in your voice.''

"Well, sure, but that's pretty normal, don't you think?"

"Not in my family.''

John heard the bitterness in Shelley's voice and remembered vaguely something Cathy had said one day when he'd made a comment about how much she did for Shelley. Something about how Shelley's parents weren't very supportive and how she didn't see much of them. "Your parents don't live in Houston, do they?"

She shook her head. Her face was in profile, so he couldn't really see her expression, but something about the slight stiffness of her body told him this was a sticky subject. "No, they live in Colorado. That's where I'm from."

"I didn't know that." Maybe Cathy had mentioned it, but he probably hadn't been paying attention. "Where in Colorado?"

"Colorado Springs."

"It's nice there."

"Yes, it's . . . a really pretty place."

"Why'd you leave?"

"I had to." Now she faced him, her gray eyes enigmatic. "It was a matter of survival."

"I don't understand."

"It's not complicated. I just had to get away from my family, and especially from my ex. I needed a fresh start. I needed to get away from the reminders of what a stupid fool I'd been."

"That bad, huh?"

She nodded, biting her bottom lip.

"You want to talk about it?"

She shook her head. "No. Not today." Turning, she made an obvious effort to shake herself free of whatever memories their conversation had stirred. "Talking about Barry is a downer. I don't want to spoil our day."

He would have liked to keep talking. He would have liked to continue getting to know her. His curiosity was aroused now, and he wished he'd paid more attention when Cathy had talked about Shelley.

He reached over to squeeze her hand. "If you don't want to talk about it, that's fine. Anyway, I see the kids coming, so what do you say? Ready to join them again?"

Chapter Five

"Mmm," Shelley said, licking her lips. "It's been a long time since I've had funnel cake."

"Good, isn't it?" John said.

Shelley couldn't remember when she'd had so much fun. So far the day had been nearly perfect. John had turned out to be an ideal companion, and she thought he was enjoying himself as much as she was.

Except for that brief period when he'd asked her about her family, there had been no discordant notes to the day. She was grateful he hadn't pushed her for more information. Maybe someday she would be able to discuss her past without pain and bitterness, but not yet.

"So what do you kids want to do next?" John asked.

The four of them were walking slowly, savoring their treat.

"I want to ride the XLR8 again," Patrick said.

"Me, too," Missy said.

John groaned, and Shelley laughed. Just then, startling her, an urgent *beep, beep* emitted from her tote.

"What's that?" John said.

"My beeper." Shelley dug it out of the tote. Darn! Why had she brought the stupid thing, anyway? Habit, she guessed. She pushed the message button and grimaced. "It's my office. Darn. I'll have to call them back. It might be important. I'd better find a phone."

John frowned but didn't comment. The kids were oblivious, skipping on ahead, talking excitedly about the XLR8. Shelley looked at John, wondering if he was irritated about her being beeped, but he wasn't looking at her.

A few dozen yards to her left, Shelley saw a telephone booth and, avoiding John's eyes, walked toward it. She dropped her quarter in the slot and punched in the office number.

"This is Shelley. You beeped me?"

"Oh, yeah, Ginny wants you," the weekend receptionist said. "I'll get her."

A few seconds later, Ginny Singer said, "Shelley? Oh, thank God!"

"What's wrong?"

"The Van Doren sale is falling apart, that's what's wrong."

Shelley swallowed. "What happened?"

"Well, you know the inspector went out there today."

"Yes."

Ginny sighed noisily. "He says the upstairs air conditioner needs replacing. Well, the Wallaces are refusing to do it. And now Mrs. Van Doren is furious and threatening to back out. I don't know what to do. Neither one of them will budge an inch."

"Oh, for crying out loud. What does a new air-conditioning unit cost, anyway? A few thousand dollars? I can't believe the Wallaces would balk over such a piddling amount. It's a drop in the bucket compared to the amount of money they're going to make on the house."

"I know, I know...."

"Did you explain to them that we were really lucky to find someone who wanted that monstrosity and was willing to give them a price so close to what they were asking?"

"Yes, Shelley, of course I did. I don't know what their problem is. They're just being stupid."

"And how did Mrs. Van Doren find out about them refusing to replace the unit, anyway?" Shelley said furiously. Celia Van Doren was *her* client. She should have been the one to talk to her.

"I didn't tell her, if that's what you're implying," Ginny said. "Walter did."

"Oh." Walter Shaver was the owner/broker of their agency.

"And he didn't have a choice. The inspector told Mrs. Van Doren about the air conditioner, and she called here, and when she found out you weren't working today, she asked to speak to Walter."

Shelley sighed. *Damn!*

"Shelley, you've got to do something. We can't lose this sale. God, I've already spent part of my commission!"

Shelley started to say something about counting chickens, but she didn't, because she felt just as desperate as Ginny. More, even. She had more at stake than Ginny did. Ginny was married to a dentist. She didn't have the financial pressures Shelley had. "I know, but I can't do anything right this minute. I'll, uh, call Mrs. Van Doren and see if we can't meet in the morning."

"The morning will be too late! She's mad. She said she's coming over here at five and she's insisting we give her the earnest money back."

Shelley looked at her watch. It was three-fifteen. What should she do?

"You need to be here when she gets here," Ginny insisted.

Shelley glanced outside the booth. John stood a few feet away, the kids a few feet beyond him. She bit her bottom lip.

"Shelley..."

"Oh, all *right*. I'll be there."

She slowly replaced the receiver. She would rather walk on hot coals than have to go out there and tell John and the kids they'd have to leave so early. But what else could she do? She simply couldn't lose this sale. It meant too much to her and Missy.

Unless John could stay with the kids...

No. She couldn't ask John to stay.

But they *did* have both their cars...and he'd been planning to stay until this evening, anyway....

She walked outside.

"Is something wrong?" John said as she approached.

She quickly explained. "I'm so sorry about this. I hate to cut the day short for the kids, but I have to leave. I just don't have a choice." She waited, hoping he'd offer to stay. He didn't. "I'm sorry," she said again.

"Oh, *Mom,* do we *have* to go?" Missy said.

"Why can't *you* stay with us, Dad?" Patrick said. "*You* don't hafta go anywhere."

Missy's eyes lit up. "Oh, Mr. Taylor, *would* you?"

John looked at Shelley, then looked at the kids. "Yes," he said, "I'll stay. But if you kids don't mind, I'd like to talk to Missy's mother for a minute in private, okay?"

He took Shelley's arm and walked her out of earshot.

"Just what would you have done if I hadn't been here?" he asked coldly.

Stung by his implication, Shelley's voice hardened. "I'd have brought Patrick home, then gone to the office and taken Missy with me. If there'd been no one at your house, I'd have taken them *both* with me. What did you *think* I'd do? Leave them here alone?"

He stared at her for a long moment, then said tightly, "I don't know what to think where you're concerned. I don't understand you. Your priorities are totally screwed up. You'd think that just this once Missy would be more important to you than that damned job of yours!"

"It's *because* of Missy that my job is so important to me," Shelley pointed out while trying to hold onto her temper. "Because I want to give her a decent life! Surely *that's* not too complicated for you to understand."

"Look, Shelley, I know that. But kids need more than material things."

She stared at him. "That's so easy for you to say, isn't it?" She shook her head. "I don't know why I'm trying to explain. Obviously, we live in different worlds. How could you possibly understand? You've never had to worry a day in your life about meeting a rent payment or putting food on the table or getting your kids' teeth fixed or anything else, for that matter."

"I've had to worry about plent—"

"Forget it," she said, cutting him off. "I was beginning to think you were really a pretty decent guy, but I can see my initial impression was right. You're nothing but a smug, superior, judgmental man who thinks he knows everything. For your information, the sale I made last weekend is falling apart, and if I lose it, I'll have to work twice as hard with even longer hours to make up for it. I *have* to go today, and if you don't want to stay with the kids, I'll take Missy with me, and you can take Patrick home with you."

Without waiting for him to answer, she stalked off. Oh! She was so angry! God, he was infuriating! She gritted her teeth and told herself to calm down. It wouldn't do to let the kids see how mad she was. "Listen, kids," she said when she reached them. "It looks as if Mr. Taylor doesn't really—"

"I said I'd stay with them, and I will," John said, walking up behind her. His voice was stiff, his eyes cool. "I don't want *their* day ruined." The word *too* shimmered in the air between them, unsaid but implied.

Shelley wanted to tell him to go stuff himself. She wanted to say thanks but no thanks. She wanted to grab Missy's hand and leave and never have to see John again.

She took a deep breath, turned and met his gaze squarely. "Thank you." Then she bent down and gave Missy a hug. "Bye, sweetie. I'll see you later. I'll try to come back to the park, okay?"

Missy smiled and returned her hug. "Sure, Mom, I understand. Don't worry." In a whisper, she said, "Remember your stomach."

As Shelley hurriedly left the park, she told herself it was pretty sad when an eight-year-old child had more maturity, open-mindedness and understanding than a thirty-some-year-old man.

She also told herself she was a fool to have been taken in by John's charming act in the first place. Obviously, the charm was a facade.

Were all men like that? she wondered as she drove out of the parking lot faster than she should have. Charming when you did what they wanted you to and complete bastards when you didn't?

Once again, she saw the accusing look in John's eyes. The look that told her she wasn't a good person. That she wasn't a good mother.

Oh, God, she was so tired of never measuring up! Of never being good enough. She didn't need this. She darned sure didn't need to be around another man who tried to make her feel bad about herself.

But mixed in with her anger was hurt and regret and twinges of guilt that she didn't want to acknowledge.

She was hurt because John hadn't tried to understand her situation. She felt regret because the perfect day and her budding friendship with John both lay in ruins. And she felt guilt because no matter how much she told herself that her leaving was unavoidable, a part of her said a good mother would never have been put in this situation to begin with.

Why did this have to happen?

Shelley sighed heavily. Maybe it was a good thing this had happened today. She was beginning to like John too much. Now, at least, she knew what he was really like. Before it was too late.

"Your dad's mad at my mom," Missy said as she and Patrick rode the Serpent together. She had to shout to make herself heard over the noise of the ride and the squeals and laughter of the riders.

"I know," Patrick shouted back.

"What're we gonna do?"

"I think we should forget about it."

"Patrick! Don't you *want* to get them together?"

"I don't know. They always end up fighting."

Missy thought for a minute. "Maybe we should talk to your Aunt Froggie."

Patrick looked skeptical. "What can she do?"

"Give us advice," Missy said as the ride slowed to a crawl, then stopped altogether.

"But, Missy, maybe this isn't such a good idea."

"Of course, it's a good idea," Missy said implacably.

Patrick sighed. It was useless to argue, and he knew it. "Okay, we'll talk to Aunt Froggie. When do you wanna do it?"

"How about tomorrow?"

"I don't think we can tomorrow, 'cause I think we're going over to my uncle Mark's house."

"Well then, we'll do it Monday. After school." Missy smiled happily as she and Patrick rejoined his father and they headed toward the next ride.

Shelley made a beeline for Ginny's office as soon as she reached the agency.

Ginny rolled her eyes. "This is a fine mess, isn't it? Got any brilliant ideas?"

"Well, on the way over here, I was thinking. How would you feel about splitting the cost of the air-conditioning unit and having it deducted from our commission?"

Ginny's eyes widened. She slowly grinned. "Shoot, I don't care. If doing that will save the sale, I say let's go for it. I mean, as you pointed out, the cost of a new unit is piddling compared to what we stand to lose if this deal falls apart."

"That's what I think. But first let's see if we can't get the Wallaces and Mrs. Van Doren to agree to split the cost."

Shelley spent the next forty-five minutes talking to the inspector and getting some estimates on the cost of a high-efficiency unit, which was what he felt the house needed, then waiting while Ginny talked to the Wallaces.

"No dice," Ginny said after hanging up. "They just won't budge. So I guess it's up to you and me."

When Shelley and Ginny told Walter Shaver, their broker, what they'd decided to do, he surprised them by saying, "If this deal falls through, the agency has even more to lose than you two, so tell you what…I'll kick in for half the new unit and you gals can pay one-quarter each.''

And that's the way it ended up. Mrs. Van Doren quickly backed off her demand for a return of her earnest money when Shelley told her what had been decided.

By six-thirty, Shelley was on her way back to Astroworld, crisis averted. She thought about how easily they'd fixed the problem, then her thoughts naturally gravitated to John again. The anger she'd managed to tamp down while she'd been dealing with the Van Doren problem resurfaced, and she found herself rehashing the harsh words she and John had exchanged.

Once more she reminded herself how lucky she was that she'd discovered John's true colors before getting any more involved with him. There was no way she would allow herself to have a relationship with a man who constantly found fault with her. She'd had more than enough of that with Barry. But no matter how many times she repeated the thought, she couldn't rid herself of her hurt and disappointment. It was going to be difficult to get through the rest of the day without showing her feelings, but she'd have to try.

She got back to the park at seven-fifteen. She'd had her hand stamped when she left, so she didn't have to pay again. She began to walk around, looking first in the areas of the rides she knew the kids liked best. She walked and walked and walked. At eight-thirty, she still hadn't found them. Her feet hurt and her head hurt, and she wasn't sure what to do. She decided she'd give it until nine, and if she hadn't found them by then, she'd go home because the park was only open until ten, so there was no sense in staying any longer.

At nine, dejected and tired, she headed back to the parking lot and drove home.

How had a day that had started out to be so promising become so frustrating and disappointing?

When she arrived home, she walked to the living room and gazed out the front window. John's house seemed to look back at her with the same disapproving gaze John had given her earlier.

Maybe you are *a bad mother....*

Tears stung her eyes. Damn him! Damn him for making her doubt herself.

For the next hour, while she waited for John and the children to return, she battled her inner demons. And finally, about ten-thirty, she managed to achieve a measure of calm and objectivity.

She vowed she would keep it. When John arrived, she would be polite but cool. She would not lose her temper again, no matter what he said or did. And she would *not* let him make her feel bad about herself.

At eleven, she heard a car pulling into the driveway. She looked out the front window. It was John and the kids. She reminded herself once more of how she planned to act, then walked outside. It was a beautiful night, but she hardly noticed. She was totally focused on her goal.

"Mom!" Missy said, climbing out of the car. "We had so much fun! Me and Patrick rode XLR8 six more times after you left! It was cool!"

"That's nice, sweetie," Shelley said, walking around to the driver's side of the car. John rolled his window down. "Thanks for staying with them. I appreciate it." Her voice was cool. She had decided not to mention going back to the park and looking all over for them. Knowing John, he would think she was just looking for sympathy or trying to make herself look better.

"You're welcome." His voice was equally cool.

"I'll see you tomorrow, Patrick!" Missy said. "'Night, Mr. Taylor."

"Good night, Missy." John's gaze met Shelley's again. "Good night."

"Good night."

And then he was backing out of their drive and pulling into his own.

"I'm so sorry about having to leave early." Shelley put her arm around Missy as they walked inside. "I *did* go back, though, but I couldn't find you."

"You did? Gee, I'm sorry."

"No, sweetie, *I'm* the one who's sorry."

"Don't feel bad, Mom. I'm not mad." Missy frowned. "Patrick's dad was mad, though, wasn't he?"

Damn. "What makes you say that?"

Missy shrugged. "I could tell. Why was he mad, Mom?"

"I guess he didn't understand why I had to go."

Missy nodded. "Are you mad at him, too?"

Shelley hesitated. "No, not anymore."

"But you were mad before?"

"Yes."

Missy thought about this for a minute. Finally she looked up, giving Shelley a shy smile tinged with hope.

"I'm glad, 'cause I like Patrick's dad, and I don't want you to be mad at him."

Later that night, as Shelley lay in bed, she kept thinking about Missy and that hopeful smile. Shelley knew she was going to have to talk to Missy about John, because it was now quite obvious what the child was hoping for. And Shelley was going to have to disabuse her of that hope because there was no way Shelley and John would ever have the kind of relationship Missy wanted them to have.

Once again, Shelley thought about Barry and what he had done to his child. It was because of his neglect that Missy was so desperately seeking a father somewhere else.

The sins of the fathers . . .

Just before Shelley fell asleep she decided she would call Barry tomorrow and give him a piece of her mind about Missy's birthday. It probably wouldn't do any good, but at least it would make her feel better.

No, you can't do that. How will that help Missy? What you need to do is be nice to him. Pretend it's only natural that he might forget Missy's birthday. Try to get him to call Missy so that she'll think he cares about her. That's what you need to do! It doesn't matter whether you feel better. It only matters that Missy feels better.

"Okay, okay," Shelley muttered aloud. "I'll be so sweet he'll think I'm a sugar cube."

Although John had gotten over his anger at Shelley by the time he and the kids left Astroworld, seeing her when he dropped Missy off had caused it to flare again.

Where did she get off acting like the injured party, anyway? he asked himself as he pulled into his own driveway. He ignored the prickle of guilt creeping along his neck.

Froggie walked into the kitchen as John and Patrick entered the house. "Hi! Did you two have a good time?"

"Yeah!" Patrick said. "It was cool." He launched into a rapid-fire recital of all the rides they'd gone on, giving her hand motions and sound effects.

When he finally wound down, Froggie said, "And how about you, John? Did you have a good time, too?"

"Sure."

Froggie's shrewd eyes narrowed. She looked as if she wanted to say more, but she didn't, and John was grateful.

An hour later, with Patrick in bed, and she and John by themselves in the TV room, she reintroduced the subject. "Did something happen today?" she asked.

"Happen?"

"Yes. You didn't sound too enthusiastic when I asked you about your day."

John hadn't meant to tell her but found himself doing it, anyway. "See?" he finished. "I was right about her all the time."

"John," Froggie said softly. "That wasn't very nice of you."

"What do you mean?" His voice was harsher than he'd intended because he already felt guilty about his behavior and her gentle admonishment just reinforced those feelings.

"You know what I mean. You should never judge someone else until you've walked in their shoes."

"You think it's okay for her to always put her job first?"

"I don't think she always puts her job first."

"She sure did today."

"I don't think so. I think what she did today was weigh the cost of losing a potential sale against the cost of momentarily disappointing her daughter. As Shelley pointed out, she has to worry about paying the rent and feeding her family and providing Missy with the necessities of life. That has to be a top priority. Was Missy upset with her?"

"No."

"Was Patrick?"

"No."

"Well, I think you overreacted," Froggie said. "And I think you owe Shelley an apology."

Maybe Froggie was right. Maybe he *had* overreacted. Maybe he *did* owe Shelley an apology.

Maybe he'd go over to her house in the morning and tell her he was sorry. The moment he decided that's what he'd do, he began to feel better.

Shelley got her opportunity to call Barry on Sunday afternoon. Missy had been invited to go to a movie with one of her school friends, and the moment she was out the door, Shelley headed for the phone. She took a deep breath and punched in the numbers.

"Hello?" said a soft, female voice.

Shelley recognized the voice as belonging to Barry's new wife. "Karen?"

"Yes."

"Karen, this is Shelley. May I speak with Barry, please?"

Shelley could almost feel the drop in temperature at the other end of the line when she identified herself.

"Just a moment," Karen said without a trace of friendliness.

Shelley could just imagine what Barry had told Karen about her. Since he would never imagine himself to be wrong about anything, he would have to make Shelley the bad guy in their marriage.

She heard a muffled conversation. Karen probably had her hand over the phone. A few minutes later, Barry said, "Hello, Shelley."

"Hello, Barry."

"What can I do for you?"

Shelley almost forgot her vow not to say anything nasty, but she caught herself in time. "Well, I know how busy you are and I figured it probably just slipped your mind, but Thursday was Missy's birthday."

"And?"

"*And?*" Shelley said, her voice inching up a notch. "*And* she didn't hear from you."

"What's your point?"

All Shelley's good resolutions flew out the window in the face of his indifference. "Barry! Missy is your daughter! It hurt her that you didn't call or send a card or a gift. She *loves* you, for God's sake. How can you just ignore her?"

"Let's get this straight once and for all," he said coldly. "I pay a ridiculous amount in child support—under protest, I might add—and I do not intend to spend another cent on a kid I'm not even sure is mine."

Shelley's mouth dropped open.

"I've had my suspicions for a long time," he continued. "She hasn't got a single one of my characteristics. In fact, she's exactly like you."

Rage nearly choked Shelley. "You bastard!" she spat. "You know damned well that Missy is your child. Why, even if I'd *wanted* to cheat on you when we were married, you had me so beaten down I wouldn't have had the confidence or the guts to do it! How you can deny a wonderful child like Missy is beyond me. And personally, I'm damned glad she's nothing like you, because frankly, you're worse than a bastard! You're a monster!" Without giving him a chance to reply, she slammed down the phone and promptly burst into furious tears.

Chapter Six

John restlessly prowled the house Sunday afternoon. He couldn't seem to settle down to anything. The Cowboys game was on TV, but he couldn't even get interested in that, and normally he would've been thrilled to have a quiet afternoon of uninterrupted football.

But not today.

Today his thoughts kept circling around Shelley and the harsh words they'd exchanged yesterday. He kept thinking about what Froggie had said to him the previous evening and about his decision to apologize to Shelley.

He finally decided he might as well get it over with. He had no excuse for delaying. Froggie was out with friends, and the kids were spending the day at his brother's.

He got up and peered out the front window. Shelley's car was in her driveway.

She's home.

Girding himself, hoping she would accept his apology without any lingering hard feelings, he walked across the street and rang the doorbell.

He waited and waited.

No one came.

John shifted uneasily. Was Shelley not answering because she knew it was him and didn't want to talk to him? Should he ring again? Or should he leave?

Don't be ridiculous. Maybe she's out back or something. Maybe she didn't hear the bell. Ring it again.

He reached over. Before he could press the bell, the door opened. Shelley stood framed in the doorway. John took one look at her swollen, red-rimmed eyes and knew something was drastically wrong.

"What do *you* want?" she said tightly, giving him no chance to speak. "I don't need anyone else telling me what a rotten parent I am. If that's what you've come for, go away."

If he hadn't realized how upset she was, he might have been tempted to answer her in kind. Instead he kept his voice gentle. "I didn't come over to tell you you're a rotten parent. I came to apologize."

She stared at him, her throat working, and he knew she was fighting tears.

"May I come in?"

Her lower lip trembled, and she made a visible effort to gather her control. "All right."

He followed her into the living room, where she suddenly stopped and swung around to face him, her gray eyes filled with anguished torment. "Look, I'm not in too good a shape right now...."

"I can see that."

"So say what you have to say and then go, okay?"

Easy does it. Remember, she's upset. "I'm very sorry for what happened yesterday," he said. "I had no right to say what I did. I was wrong. Can you forgive me?"

She swallowed, and the tears that were so close to the surface brimmed over. Her hand shook as she brushed them away. She nodded wordlessly, obviously too distraught to answer.

John acted instinctively, the same way he would have if it had been his daughter or his sister or his mother who needed comfort. He reached out and gathered Shelley close, patting her head and saying, "Hey, it's okay."

She let him hold her for a few moments, then pulled away. Keeping her eyes averted, she said, "I—I'm sorry. I'm acting like an idiot."

"No, you're not." He touched her arm. "C'mon. Let's go sit on the couch."

She allowed him to lead her over to the dark blue sofa facing the fireplace.

After they were seated, he said, "Do you want to talk about it?"

She looked at him, searching his face. She must have seen whatever it was she sought because she shrugged and said, "Are you sure you want to hear this? It's an ugly story."

"I don't care." He reached for her hand and clasped it firmly, pleased when she let him hold it without pulling away.

She began to talk, haltingly at first, then more rapidly. John listened in growing horror. How could anyone say such lousy things about her and Missy? When she got to the part where Barry had denied parentage of his daughter, John clenched his teeth. Damn, the guy was a real son of a bitch. No wonder Shelley was so quick to take offense when she was criticized. If this was the kind of thing she'd had to put up with over the years, John didn't blame her for being defensive.

Now John felt even more ashamed of his own recent actions. Although he'd added to her problems unknowingly, he had still contributed to her unhappiness, especially when he'd implied she wasn't a good mother.

"So then I hung up on him," Shelley finished. Her eyes, calmer now, met John's. "And you know what, John? I decided that's the last time I'm ever contacting Barry again. If this is the way he wants it, this is the way it's going to be. Missy'll be better off without him if he's going to treat her like this."

John squeezed her hand.

"I'll make it up to her," she continued, speaking as if to herself. "I'll be such a good mother, she won't even miss having a father."

John wished he knew what to say. He wished he had the ability to put words together that would erase the pain he knew Shelley felt. The best he could come up with was, "You're absolutely right. The best thing is to forget about him. He doesn't deserve one more minute of your thoughts. Just put the whole ugly episode out of your mind."

"Easier said than done," she said wryly.

Her smile was crooked, but it was a smile, and John felt encouraged by her attempt. "Tell you what," he suggested, "how about a complete change of scenery? How about if I take you somewhere really nice for dinner tonight? Have you ever been to the Rainbow Lodge?"

She shook her head. "I can't go out tonight."

"Why not?"

"I don't have anyone to sit with Missy."

"That's no problem. She can come over and spend the evening with Froggie and the kids. We'll let 'em get Burger King or something. In fact, she can even spend the night. Nikki will be ecstatic. She's got a bad case of hero worship, you know."

"You don't want to take me out. I—I'm not exactly a barrel of laughs right now."

"I don't expect you to be a barrel of laughs. We'll just go out, have dinner, talk a little bit. It'll be nice. Come on. Say yes."

She sighed deeply. "Oh, all right, I'll go." Now her smile was more genuine. "I'll try not to make you sorry you asked me."

John stood, bringing her to her feet. He smiled down at her. "I promise. I'm not going to be sorry. I'll make reservations for seven-thirty."

"Okay."

Her eyes were still shadowed, and sympathy for her caused him to lean over and brush her cheek with his lips. In that brief moment of contact, he caught a whiff of a light, flowery fragrance, which produced a sharp ache in the vicinity of his heart, because it reminded him of Cathy. As he straightened, his gaze met Shelley's.

Suddenly he felt awkward, and he could see she did, too. He tried to cover the awkwardness with an attempt at humor. "Now, no more crying. I don't want a red-eyed date tonight."

She made a face. "I'll just have to wear red and be color-coordinated, I guess."

They both laughed, and the moment passed.

She walked him to the door. "Thanks, John. I appreciate your listening."

"Anytime."

After John left, Shelley berated herself for crying all over him. God, it was bad enough Barry was such a lowlife, but to have other people know about it! Yet John hadn't seemed to think less of Shelley when she'd told him what Barry had said and how she'd reacted. In fact, John had supported her actions.

You should have been stronger, though. You should have been able to handle this situation with Barry on your own.

But it had felt so good to have someone's shoulder to lean on. And not just any someone, either, she finally admitted as she straightened up the house and did some laundry. It felt good to lean on John.

You're getting too attached to him. You know that, don't you?

She stopped in the middle of folding a bath towel and stared off into space. She *was* getting too attached to him. And those kinds of feelings were dangerous. He would never be interested in someone like her. Never. Not after Cathy. So even if Shelley wanted a relationship—which she didn't—she would end up getting hurt if she indulged herself in these feelings.

You shouldn't be going out with him tonight, either. Not only because it's asking for trouble to spend too much time with him but because it's going to give Missy the wrong idea....

Sure enough, when Shelley told Missy—as casually as she could manage—that she was going out to dinner with John, Missy's eyes lit up.

"Oh, Mom! Cool! And I can spend the night at Patrick's house? *Really?*"

"Yes, really."

"Gee, I'm glad you and Patrick's dad aren't mad at each other anymore."

"We weren't mad at each other."

Missy gave her a look that said, *c'mon, Mom, do you think I'm stupid?*

"Well, maybe a little..." Shelley conceded.

Missy grinned. "I'm glad you're goin' out, Mom."

Shelley wanted to say, *it's not a date,* yet how could she? If she tried to explain why John had asked her out, she'd have to say she was upset, and then Missy would wonder why. No, better to let Missy think whatever she wanted to think...at least for now.

When it was time to get ready for the evening, Shelley debated over what to wear. If she wanted to keep the tone of the evening friendship only—which she knew was the most sensible thing to do—she should wear a suit or something similar. But Shelley didn't want to. They were going to the Rainbow Lodge, and she'd never been there before, and it was a really nice place. And Shelley had so little opportunity to dress up.

What could it hurt, just this one time, to wear something feminine and pretty? She ignored the little warning voice inside that said she was making a big mistake and selected a short, black silk crepe dress with a low, square-cut neckline. With it she wore big diamond-shaped black earrings studded with gold rhinestones and, instead of wearing her hair in the smooth chignon she normally favored, she tied it back loosely with a black velvet ribbon.

"Gee, Mom, you look pretty!" Missy said enthusiastically.

Shelley smiled, buried her misgivings, and together, they walked across the street.

John's mouth went dry when he saw Shelley. He couldn't get over how different she looked. How *sexy!* It took all his willpower to keep his voice from betraying his thoughts as he greeted her and Missy.

"Nice dress," he said, smiling down at her.

"Thanks." A becoming pink stained her cheeks. All traces of the afternoon's unhappiness had vanished. She looked relaxed and beautiful. Too beautiful for his peace of mind, he was afraid. "The kids are in the TV room," he told Missy.

She grinned and headed in that direction.

"Let me just say goodbye to Froggie and the kids, and then we can be off," he said.

"I'll come say goodbye, too," Shelley said.

John was acutely conscious of her as they walked toward the back of the house. He could smell her perfume—that same light scent he'd noticed earlier. Suddenly he felt nervous, like a kid going on his first date. The situations weren't dissimilar, he thought dryly. He hadn't had a date in so long, he might as well be on his first. In fact, after he and Cathy started going together as juniors in high school, he'd never dated another girl.

Almost twenty years. He didn't know how to act.

As they entered the room, Froggie looked up and smiled. "Hi, Shelley. Don't you look lovely?"

"Thanks."

They said their goodbyes, and John knew Froggie was studying him. He wondered what she was thinking. When he'd told her he'd invited Shelley to dinner, he'd emphasized that he'd felt Shelley needed to get out. He'd made it sound as if the only reason he'd asked her to dinner was to get her mind off her problems.

It wasn't the only reason, and John knew it.

And now he was sure Froggie knew it, too.

He was relieved when they finally left.

It took thirty minutes to drive to the Rainbow Lodge, which was located off Memorial Drive close to downtown. On the way, they listened to a Neville Brothers CD after John discovered Shelley enjoyed their music as much as he did. "If I could afford it," she said, "I'd go to New Orleans every couple of months. I love everything about the Cajun and Creole cultures—the music, the food, the entire way of life...."

He smiled. He felt the same way.

"Have you ever danced to Cajun music?" Shelley asked.

"No. Have you?"

"No, but I'd sure like to. Maybe one of these days."

Her voice trailed off, and John thought he heard her sigh. It struck him that Shelley had probably not had much opportunity for fun since her divorce. If he recalled correctly, she'd been divorced about five years now, and he knew—from what Cathy had told him—that Shelley had had to work full-time the whole time she went to real estate school. It couldn't have been easy. She'd juggled her job, her schooling, her child's needs, and all the responsibilities of her home almost single-handedly. And she'd had to pinch pennies to make ends meet.

Again, guilt surged through him. He decided that he would do whatever he could to make things up to her.

When they drove down the driveway leading to the fabled restaurant, Shelley said, "Oh, it's lovely!"

John smiled. Cathy had said the same thing the first time he'd brought her here. It was a nice setting, he thought, with the tiny lights strung through the trees year-round and the gazebo off to the left where countless couples had married. The restaurant had been fashioned from an old Victorian house and filled with antiques which lent it charm and authenticity. The only obvious modernization were the floor to ceiling windows installed across the back of the restaurant, which afforded diners a view of the bayou and dense forestlike foliage. If you were lucky enough to get a table by the windows, you were usually treated to the sight of possums and squirrels and the occasional raccoon frolicking on the grounds or the wraparound porch.

During the Christmas season, the restaurant was lavishly decorated, with several small trees on different levels. As he and Shelley entered the restaurant and waited for the hostess to seat them, Shelley continued to give little sounds of pleasure as she looked around.

"John, this is wonderful," she murmured, eyes shining.

It gave John a strange feeling to know he was responsible for putting that light in her eyes. The feeling was part pleasure—he was glad he'd made her forget about that pond scum ex-husband of hers—and part disquiet because even though he'd said he wasn't going to, here he was, taking on Shelley's problems.

That's what friends do. They care.

"Mr. Taylor?" the hostess said, breaking into his thoughts. "Your table's ready."

John had asked for a table by the windows, and he was glad of his foresight when he saw Shelley's delighted reaction.

After they'd placed their drink order, Shelley leaned back in her chair and gazed out the window. "Oh, look! There's a possum!" she exclaimed. "Oh, how cute!" She continued in this vein for several minutes, then turned her shining eyes back to him. "This was a great idea—coming here."

John smiled. "I'm glad you're enjoying it."

"I wouldn't even care if the food was terrible, although I know it won't be." She laughed. "You're probably thinking I don't get out much if I get this excited over dinner at a nice restaurant."

He shrugged. "I don't get out that much myself since Cathy died." For the first time in three years, saying her name didn't hurt and didn't cause that familiar ache of sadness.

"She used to love to come here, didn't she? I remember her talking about this place and Brennan's." Her expression softened. "I feel very flattered that

you'd bring me here, John. It must be hard...
remembering other, happier times."

"You know, it's funny," he admitted, "but I don't
feel sad tonight."

"Don't you? I'm glad."

"Yes," he said slowly. "I am, too." In that moment, he realized that he'd been clinging to his sadness just as a child would cling to a familiar toy at
bedtime.

Their gazes locked as this realization washed over
him. Something—some emotion John couldn't describe—arced across the table between them.

For the rest of the evening, while they drank their
wine and ate their dinner of poached salmon, tiny new
potatoes and fresh asparagus, and their dessert of
chocolate mousse accompanied by fragrant cups of
coffee, while they talked and laughed and pretended
they were simply friends out for a casual evening—
that same awareness shimmered in the air between
them like the lights in the trees outside their window
shimmered in the velvety night.

It was nearly ten before they left the restaurant. As
they waited for the valet parking attendant to bring
around John's car, Shelley looked up at him and said,
"Thank you, John. This was just what I needed."

"You're very welcome." He wanted to tell her that
he'd needed this, too, but he thought he'd better not.
First he needed to sort out his emotions.

They were both quiet on the way home, but it was a
contented, comfortable silence. An easy-listening sta-
tion played softly on the radio, and it seemed like no

time at all before John was pulling into Shelley's driveway.

He turned off the engine and cut the lights. Silence settled around them. "Well," she said, turning toward him, "thanks again. It was a wonderful evening." She reached for the door handle.

"Wait...I'll walk you to the door." He was glad when she didn't protest. She even waited until he'd gotten out and come around to her side to open her door.

They walked slowly along the walkway, stopping next to the tall crepe myrtle that marked the side of the front entrance. The slightly cool night air held the scent of rain, and off in the distance, John saw lightning streak the sky.

"I guess everyone's asleep at your house," Shelley said.

John looked across the street. His house was dark. "Yes. Froggie goes to bed early. She says she needs her beauty sleep." He chuckled, turning his gaze back to Shelley. "But I think the real reason is the kids wear her out."

"Yes, I'm sure they do. They'd wear me out, and I'm a lot younger. Speaking of kids, in the morning, be sure and send Missy home for breakfast, okay? Froggie's done enough by watching her tonight."

"Froggie wouldn't mind giving her breakfast, but if you want her home, we'll send her."

"Well...I guess I'd better go in. I need my beauty sleep, too." As she spoke, a slight breeze ruffled her hair and sent a whiff of her light fragrance drifting toward John, bringing with it something even more potent.

John's breath caught. Afterwards, he was never sure how it happened. Suddenly, without conscious thought, he drew her into his arms. She raised her face, and he lowered his. When their lips met, softly, she sighed. Her breath was sweet, her mouth warm and yielding under his.

Something powerful rocketed through him, and he tightened his arms around her, fitting her to him so that he could feel every womanly curve. He deepened the kiss, and she instantly responded, allowing him the access he craved.

Desire, swift and heated, surged through him. It had been so long . . . so long. . . .

But even as he acknowledged the wanting, even as his body cried out for more, a kernel of reason remained. This was madness. This was asking for trouble. Regretfully, he ended the kiss.

They looked at each other. Her eyes were luminous in the moonlight, and she was breathing just as hard and as fast as he was. He started to say he was sorry, then he stopped. Maybe it was best to say nothing. She could be hurt, and he didn't want to hurt her. She'd been hurt enough.

"Good night, Shelley," he whispered. He brushed her cheek with his fingers.

She covered his hand with her own for a brief moment. "Good night, John."

Then she turned away and let herself into the house.

Shelley leaned against the door and closed her eyes. She could hear the sound of the ignition as John started his car and drove out of the driveway and across the street.

Her heart was pounding. She could still feel the imprint of John's lips against her own. Her thoughts tumbled around and around.

She'd wanted him to kiss her.

She'd wanted it very much.

But now that he had, things were so much more difficult than they had been before. Because nothing had really changed. John was still John. When, and if, he married again, it would be to a woman similar to Cathy.

And Shelley was nothing like Cathy. And she never would be.

If Shelley allowed herself to care for John too much, she would get hurt. Badly.

What was she going to do? She knew she had to get their relationship back to what it had been. Friends only.

How was she going to do that now? After she'd shown him by her reaction to him and his kiss that she desired him sexually?

After long moments of berating herself for her weakness in allowing the kiss to happen, she finally headed toward her bedroom.

Oh, God, how was she going to face him tomorrow? She would be so embarrassed. The memory of how she'd kissed him caused her face to flame.

What's done was done. She couldn't undo the kiss.

But maybe she could practice some damage control. If, when she next saw John, she pretended nothing had happened—if she acted as if the kiss was no big deal—maybe then they could go back to their old footing.

Sure, it might be awkward for a while, but they'd get past it. They *had* to get past it.

Because there was no other option open to them.

If they didn't get past it, Shelley would have to avoid John's company completely. And how could she do that? They lived across the street from each other, and their children were best friends.

No. Treating this episode as if it never happened was the only thing to do.

Chapter Seven

John couldn't go to sleep. He kept remembering the feel of Shelley's body, the sweetness of her mouth, and how she'd made him feel.

He shouldn't have kissed her. He knew that. It was madness. He didn't know what he'd been thinking.

That's the trouble. You weren't thinking. Your hormones were thinking for you....

Was that it? Was that why he'd kissed her? Had he been without a woman for so long that all it took was someone soft and willing, for him to lose all control and common sense?

Maybe that was part of it, but it wasn't the whole reason. He cared for Shelley. He could deny it all he wanted, but she'd gotten under his skin.

He'd been wrong about her. He'd thought she was cold and tough—a real man-eater. She was anything but. That coolness was just a facade, a shield she wore to protect her from people she was afraid would hurt her. Today she'd shown him the extent of her vulnerability when she'd confided in him, and in so doing, she'd aroused all his protective instincts.

Yes, he cared for her. And he liked her. She was fun. *You're attracted to her, too.*

The knowledge thrummed deep inside.

How had this happened? She was all wrong for him. They wanted different things out of life. Shelley obviously had something to prove, and John didn't. He simply wanted what he'd had before. A wife and a mother for his children. Someone who thought the most important career in the world was staying home to take care of the kids and him.

John knew it would be asking for trouble to get involved with Shelley. As a family man, the only kind of relationship he wanted—aside from friendship—was one that would lead to marriage. And since marriage to Shelley wasn't in the cards, that meant he'd better cool it with her.

That might be tough, though. The kiss had altered things between them. It would be difficult to pretend nothing had happened. He wondered if he should simply talk to Shelley about it, tell her it was a mistake on his part and could they just forget about it?

John lay on his back and stared at the ceiling as he thought about his dilemma. He finally decided he would take his cue on how to behave toward her from Shelley herself. If she acted as if the kiss was important, as if it had changed things between them, he would be forced to discuss the situation with her and tell her how he felt. If not—if she acted as if the kiss hadn't happened at all—he would do the same.

Shelley spent Monday morning on the property desk, which meant that any incoming calls about listings came to her. Unfortunately, it was a quiet morning, although just before noon, when her twice-weekly shift would end, she did get one live one. The woman, a Mrs. Medwell, agreed to let Shelley show her some houses the following afternoon. With any luck, Shelley might make another sale.

After a quick, solitary lunch at Souper Salad, Shelley did some canvassing in her territory and made a few cold calls, which yielded one possibility for a listing.

At two-thirty, she decided to call it a day and go home early. She used her car phone to call the sitter and tell her she wouldn't be needed.

"You must be a mind reader," Mrs. Dunbar said happily. "My bunco group is coming tonight, and this'll give me more time to get ready."

Since she still felt a bit guilty over leaving Astroworld early Saturday and cutting Missy's birthday celebration short, Shelley decided to make lasagna and banana cream pie for dinner, two of Missy's favorites. She was just putting the pie crust in the oven to bake when Missy came running in from school.

"Mom! What're you doing home so early?" Missy said with a pleased grin.

"Baking a banana cream pie."

"Oh, boy!" Missy ran off to her room to dump her books and change her clothes, then came skipping back to the kitchen. "Can I call Patrick and ask him to come over?"

"Don't you have homework?"

"I can do it after we eat."

"That means no TV tonight," Shelley warned.

"I don't care."

"All right."

"Thanks, Mom!"

Ten minutes later, Patrick arrived, and the two friends went off to play in the tree house. Shelley filled the pie, then made the meringue and browned it. By four-thirty, the pie was in the refrigerator and the lasagna was baking in the oven, and Shelley decided she would spend the next hour doing some much-needed weeding of the front flower beds. Although the house was a rental, Shelley took pride in the way it looked, feeling it was a reflection on her if the yard was untended. Besides, it was a beautiful day, and the fresh air called to her.

She gathered together her gardening tools, dumped them all into a bucket, and walked outside.

"Missy!" she called. "I'll be out front if you need me."

Missy poked her head out the door of the tree house. "Okay, Mom."

Shelley walked around to the front of the house. She glanced across to John's house. His car wasn't in the driveway or in the open garage. He wasn't home from work yet. Thinking about him caused her heart to speed up a little, and she immediately told herself not to be silly. *Remember what you decided. When you see him, you're going to act as if nothing has happened. Nothing.*

For the next forty-five minutes Shelley diligently weeded out the bed of impatiens that bordered the Indian hawthorn bushes fronting the house. She still wasn't quite finished, but it was time to take her lasagna out of the oven, so she got up. As she straightened, she saw John out of the corner of her eye. She turned. Sure enough, he was out front watching Nikki skate up and down on the driveway.

While she was debating whether or not to call out a greeting, he looked up and waved. She waved back. Her heart was speeding up again, which irritated her. Honestly! What was wrong with her? You'd think she'd never been kissed before.

Well, it has *been an awfully long time!*

That's me, she answered herself wryly—kiss deprived. Maybe that's like oxygen-deprived, and it affects your brain. She couldn't help laughing at the thought.

She debated whether or not to walk across the street for a moment. Thinking she might as well get this first meeting over with, she headed in his direction.

"You look like you've been working hard," he said as she approached. He smiled, but she sensed a slight awkwardness and knew he probably felt as self-conscious as she did.

"Yeah. The weeds were threatening to take over." She wished she didn't look quite so grubby. "She's doing quite well on her skates," she said, inclining her head toward Nikki.

"Now she is. She took a lot of spills when she first got them."

Nikki grinned. "Look at me, Shelley!" she called. Shelley waved and thought the tyke looked adorable with her helmet and knee and elbow pads. Like a miniature hockey player.

Just then Froggie appeared at the end of the driveway. She was all dressed up in a dark blue dress and heels. "I'm leaving now, John. Hi, Shelley!"

"Okay," he said. "See you later."

"Hi, Froggie," Shelley said.

They all moved off the driveway so Froggie could back her car out.

"Her bridge night," John said.

Suddenly Shelley knew exactly what to do to show John she wasn't the least bit embarrassed by what had happened between them last night or that it would change anything. "In that case, why don't you and the kids come have dinner with us? I've made lasagna and a banana cream pie."

For a moment, she thought he was going to refuse, but then he said, "That sounds great. Thanks."

"Give me thirty minutes, then it'll be ready."

"Okay. We'll be there."

John had almost told Shelley that Froggie had left a pot roast in the Crockpot for him and the kids. But it was obvious to him that she was trying to act as if nothing had changed between them. Her invitation had been issued with studied casualness.

Yeah, but you were supposed to be cooling it. Having dinner with her doesn't qualify . . .

"I know, I know," he muttered aloud. "But if I'd refused, she'd have thought I was embarrassed by last night or something. I wanted to show her we could go back to the way we were before, that we don't have to avoid each other or feel funny about last night. I'll gradually ease away after tonight."

Still telling himself he'd done the only thing he could do under the circumstances, he turned off the Crockpot. Later, he'd empty the contents into a big plastic container. They could eat the pot roast tomorrow night.

He washed Nikki's face and hands, then turned his attention to himself. When he caught himself considering changing clothes, he stopped short.

Casual, remember? Friends only, remember? There's no reason to change clothes.

Sheepishly, he contented himself with brushing his teeth and combing his hair.

Then he and Nikki walked across the street.

"You kids want to help set the table?" Shelley asked after giving John a beer and telling him to make himself at home while she got dinner on the table.

"Sure," Missy said.

"Okay," Patrick said.

"I wanna help, too," Nikki said.

"No, I don't think so, Nikki," John said. It was one thing to have her help out at home when they used plastic dishes, but he could see Shelley had gotten out some nice china. "You might break something."

"It's okay, John," Shelley said, her eyes meeting his. "I'd love to have her help. She'll be careful."

Nikki's little face glowed. "I'll be careful, Daddy."

"Okay, if you're sure." He leaned against the kitchen counter and sipped at his beer and watched as Shelley gently directed the kids. She wisely gave Nikki the folded napkins to place by each plate. Then she suggested Nikki help Missy put out the silverware while she set out the food.

John's gaze followed Shelley as she moved to the refrigerator and opened it. When she bent over to remove a bowl of salad, her cutoffs tightened across her rump, and John could feel his hormones betraying him again. He looked away, concentrating on watching Nikki as she carefully placed each piece of silver exactly the way Missy told her to. He smiled as he saw how his daughter caught her lower lip between her teeth. The gesture of concentration reminded him so much of Cathy, and now he felt doubly guilty for his involuntary sexual response to Shelley only minutes before.

"There," Shelley said after placing the pan of lasagna on the table. "We're all done. Good job, kids." She studied the table. "Oh, I forgot the butter."

Nikki followed Shelley over to the refrigerator, saying, "I'll put it on the table, Shelley."

"Okay, honey." She handed the dish to Nikki.

The next thing John knew, the butter dish lay smashed on the tile floor and Nikki had a horrified look on her face.

"It's okay, sweetie," Shelley said, kneeling to comfort Nikki.

"B-but I broke your dish!" Nikki wailed.

"I can get a new dish. It's no big deal. We all make mistakes. Mistakes are a part of life." Shelley's gaze met John's over Nikki's head. *It really is okay,* her eyes told him.

How patient she was, John thought as he and Shelley cleaned up the mess. How understanding of a little girl's feelings. It struck him that in her own way she was every bit as good a mother as Cathy had been.

The thought jolted him. Was he comparing Shelley with Cathy? And *favorably?* How could he? They were nothing alike.

Liar. In all the ways that count, Shelley is very much like Cathy, and you know it. She's honest, sincere, warmhearted, generous, and she loves Missy with the same intensity that Cathy loved our children.

His gaze traveled over her—over her shining hair, her slightly flushed skin, her generous mouth. The memory of how she'd felt in his arms, how eagerly she'd returned his kiss, leapt to life, bringing another hot flame of desire with it.

John hastily averted his eyes, and by the time they'd cleaned up the mess and sat back down and begun to eat, he'd managed to get himself under control again. He was determined to stay that way, and to this end, he was grateful for the presence of the kids, because they provided a diversion. With their presence, the conversation was lively and impersonal and there were no opportunities for any kind of private exchange between him and Shelley.

Unfortunately, though, John's brain had a life of its own, and he couldn't stop his thoughts from dwelling on Shelley and how different she was from his original assessment. He couldn't believe he'd gone all those years not liking her. Now he liked her far too much.

She laughed at something Patrick said, and John watched her. She had the nicest laugh, he decided. It was low and musical. More a throaty chuckle than anything else.

A bedroom laugh.

Once the thought formed, John couldn't get rid of it. All kinds of unbidden images filled his mind, and he couldn't stop himself from thinking about what Shelley would be like in bed. What it would be like to make love to her.

He kept remembering how warm and willing and passionate she'd been when he'd kissed her last night. He was glad he was sitting down, because his brain wasn't the only part of his anatomy with a life of its own.

Man, what's wrong with you? Why can't you control yourself? Remember what you decided. You're not going to make love to Shelley. Not now. Not ever. It's friendship only . . .

"This is the best lasagna I've ever eaten," he said, determined to rid himself of these completely unsuitable thoughts and feelings.

"Thanks."

How was it he'd never before realized her eyes were the exact color of the sky on a rainy day? A man could drown in those eyes. . . .

"She puts sliced meatballs in hers instead of sausage," Missy said. "And her sauce is homemade."

"Speaking of which, you have sauce on your nose, toots," Shelley said, laughing that low, throaty laugh again.

"When do you have time to make homemade sauce?" John said. He told his hormones to go back to sleep.

Shelley shrugged. "It's no big deal. I just throw a bunch of stuff in a pot and let it slow cook for a couple of hours. When I make it, I always make a big batch and freeze some. That way I have it when I need it.'' She smiled. ''I like to cook. It's relaxing.''

When they were finished with their lasagna and salad, John helped Shelley clear the table. It gave him a funny feeling, because he and Cathy had always cleaned up the kitchen together.

''Can me and Patrick go play Super Mario World?'' Missy asked, naming her current favorite video game.

''Patrick and I,'' Shelley corrected automatically. ''And no, I don't think so. We're going to have our dessert now, and then you need to go get started on your homework, remember?''

Missy sighed. ''Yeah, I remember.''

''And we need to go home,'' John said, glancing over at Nikki, who was already yawning.

Shelley removed a pie from the refrigerator. As she fixed each serving, she handed it to John. Once, their fingers touched, and he wondered if she felt the same tingle of electricity from the contact as he did.

He was relieved when they finished their pie and could leave. Being here like this, participating in this cozy little domestic scene, was too dangerous. His resolve to stay away from her, to keep their relationship one of friendship only, was weakening.

He couldn't allow that to happen.

Throughout the evening, Shelley had been wondering what John was thinking. Was he comparing her to Cathy? Finding Shelley lacking?

And then, as he was saying good-night, he'd had such a strange expression on his face. It seemed to be made up of part regret, part relief.

Well, Shelley felt relieved, too. She'd gotten through the evening without mishap. She felt as if she'd acquitted herself well. She had kept the tone of the evening friendly and nothing more.

But it had been hard. She'd been acutely aware of John across the table from her. The memory of the kiss they'd shared had never been far from the surface of her mind. She realized more than ever how attracted to him she was and knew it wouldn't take much for her to fall in love with him. The knowledge frightened her. A lot.

Even if John were a suitable candidate for a romantic relationship, she was just beginning to find her emotional feet. She simply wasn't sure she could handle the stress and uncertainty and emotional upheaval of a romantic liaison with a man who hadn't yet gotten over losing the great love of his life.

Good Lord, that's all you need! Constant comparisons to someone else. Someone who did everything right. Someone to whom you could never measure up.

By the time Shelley went to bed, she knew she'd made the only decision she could make. She believed in that verse from the Bible, the one that said there was a season for everything. Obviously, this was not the right time for her or for John. Maybe, if this attraction between them had happened a year from now, it might have worked. But right now, for Shelley at least, she needed to concentrate her energies on her career and on building a good, secure life for herself and her daughter.

But that didn't mean she and John couldn't remain friends and occasionally do something together with their kids. Surely she could handle that.

Can you? Won't it be playing with fire to spend time with him now that your feelings for him are dangerously close to crossing the line?

She sighed heavily. Maybe she should think about moving. Getting away from John completely.

Oh, for heaven's sake! You're being ridiculous. All you have to do is exercise a little self-discipline, and you'll be fine.

She could do that.

She *would* do that.

Decision made, she turned her pillow over to the cool side, closed her eyes, and went to sleep.

On Tuesday morning when Shelley arrived at the office, Wendy, the receptionist, said, "Mr. Shaver wants to see you."

Alarm pricked Shelley's spine. Oh, no, what now? Had something else happened with the Wallace house? All kinds of possibilities raced through Shelley's mind as she headed anxiously toward Walter Shaver's office.

"Shelley, come in," the older man said when she knocked on his partially open door. He smiled.

Some of Shelley's disquiet faded in the face of his cheerful expression. Surely he wouldn't look so complacent if something was wrong.

"Sit down. I wanted to talk to you about something."

Shelley sat on one of the two burgundy leather chairs flanking his desk and gave her boss an expectant look.

"You've done a terrific job since you started with the agency, Shelley." His blue eyes gleamed behind his trifocals.

A warm glow of pleasure filled Shelley at his praise. "Thank you, Walter."

"You show great promise, and I think you have a real future with Shaver Realty... if you want it."

She smiled happily. "Oh, I want it." For someone who had never been given much encouragement or praise, either by her parents or her husband, Walter's compliments were like balm to a wound.

He leaned back, tenting his hands and eyeing her thoughtfully. "You know, Lydia and I have been talking about opening a couple of branch offices— maybe one in the Woodlands and one down in Clear Lake. If we do, we're going to need good managers for them. What do you think? Would you be interested in managing an office for us?"

"Me?" Shelley said incredulously. "But I'm so new to this business, and you have other people with so much more experience."

"Doesn't matter how many years' experience you have," he said. "What matters is how you handle people, and you seem to have a knack for smoothing troubled waters and keeping everyone happy. People trust you."

Shelley positively beamed. "I'm flattered that you think so, and I would be honored to be considered for one of the management slots, Walter."

"Good," he said. "I was hoping you'd say that. It won't be any time soon. In fact, it might not happen for a year or more. But I just wanted to know if you were interested."

Shelley practically floated out of his office. No one had ever given her such a vote of confidence before, and it made her feel about ten feet tall.

For the rest of the day, every time she thought about Walter's confidence in her, she grinned. It was wonderful to have someone like Walter believing in her.

She was on her way.

Nothing could stop her now.

Chapter Eight

"Patrick," Missy said, "nothing's happening."

"What do you mean?" Patrick looked up from his math, which the two were doing together at Patrick's house.

"You know...with our *plan*."

"Oh. That."

Missy sighed and put down her pencil. "It's been two weeks, longer even, since you and your dad and Nikki had dinner at our house, and since then... nothing."

Patrick shrugged.

"I thought my mom and your dad were getting along great, didn't you?" Missy pressed.

"Well, yeah..."

"I think they really like each other now."

"Yeah..."

Missy frowned. "Then why aren't they going out on dates like they did that one night?"

Patrick shrugged again. "I dunno."

"I don't know, either, but I think we should talk to your Aunt Froggie about it. We were goin' to before, remember?"

Patrick looked dubious.

"C'mon, Patrick, don't you *want* them to get together? Don't you *want* to be my brother? Don't you *want* us to live in the same house? Think how cool that would be!"

"But Missy, maybe—"

"Let's go talk to your aunt right now," Missy said, jumping up and ignoring Patrick's obvious reluctance.

"Oh, okay..."

The two friends headed out to the kitchen. Froggie was cleaning carrots and looked around as they entered. "Done with your homework already?"

"No, but, uh, we wanted to talk to you about something," Missy said, giving Patrick a look that clearly said, *say something.*

Froggie put the paring knife she'd been using down on the counter, walked to the table and sat. "This sounds serious. What's up?"

"It *is* serious," Missy said.

Patrick shuffled his feet. "Uh, Aunt Froggie, Missy and me, we were talking, and—"

"And we think it would be really cool if my mom and Patrick's dad got married!" Missy said.

Froggie studied the two children, amusement sparking her blue eyes. "You do, huh?"

"Yeah," Missy said.

Patrick just nodded.

Fighting a smile, Froggie said, "And how do you propose to accomplish that?"

"Well," Missy said, "we thought if we could get them together enough times, they'd pro'bly fall in love like they do on TV."

Froggie grinned. "Osmosis, huh?"

Patrick frowned. "What's osmosis?"

"Never mind," Froggie said. "Actually, I agree with you. I think your mom..." she looked at Missy "...and your dad..." she looked at Patrick "...are perfect for each other."

"You *do?*" Missy said delightedly. She gave Patrick one of her I-told-you-so looks.

"But I think they're going to need some help coming to the same conclusion," Froggie continued.

"Just what we thought," Missy said.

"What kind of help?" Patrick said.

"Let me think a minute," Froggie said. "It can't be anything too obvious. If there was only some reason they needed to be together. I wonder if I could get your mother to help me do something, Missy. That way we could get her over here. Then maybe I could make myself scarce." She frowned. "I don't know what, though."

"Hmm," Missy said.

"Too bad your class doesn't have a field trip coming up. Something like that would be perfect." She gave the kids a hopeful look. "Is anything like that coming up?"

"There's the Winter Science Project," Patrick said.

"What's that?" Froggie asked.

"It's a show at the convention center where all the schools compete with different science projects," Missy explained.

Froggie shook her head. "That's no good. We need something where the parents are involved."

Missy's eyes rounded. "But the parents *are* involved in this. Just the other day Mrs. Bickham was asking for parents who could help out. I wanted to ask my mom, but since she's so busy, I didn't...but I *could!*"

"And I could ask my dad!" Patrick said.

"Then they'd *have* to spend time together, wouldn't they?" Missy said.

"*Yeah,*" Patrick echoed.

The kids gave Froggie a triumphant look.

She chuckled. "So what are you waiting for?"

John massaged his temples.

Man, he was tired! It had been a long week, and it still wasn't over. Today was only Thursday. And he had the granddaddy of all headaches!

He stood, intending to head for the lunchroom where he knew he'd find a bottle of aspirin, when his phone rang. Hoping it wasn't a customer with a billing problem, he picked it up.

It was Patrick. "Dad, can I ask you something?"

John smiled, momentarily forgetting his headache. "Sure." He sat down again.

"Remember me tellin' you about the Winter Science Project?"

"Yes." John remembered Patrick mentioning how his class was concentrating on great inventions of the twentieth century.

"Well, we need another parent to sponsor us."

John rolled his eyes. Patrick was always volunteering him to drive on field trips or help with class projects because so many of the other parents worked at jobs where they couldn't take time off.

"Will you do it, Dad?"

"What is this going to entail, Patrick? I can't spare a lot of time during the day. We're really swamped right now and will be for the next couple of months."

"You don't have to come during the day. It'll just be at night and maybe on Saturdays a little bit."

"I don't know, Patrick. I—"

"Please, Dad...we really need somebody, and I don't have a mom to ask."

John sighed. Patrick really knew how to press the right guilt buttons. "All right. You can tell Mrs. Bickham I'll do it. Or should I call her?"

"No, that's okay," Patrick said hurriedly. "I'll tell her tomorrow. She'll pro'bly be sendin' a note home or something."

After they hung up, John shook his head in amusement. Still thinking about his son and the way he could wheedle John into anything, he headed for the lunchroom. After locating the aspirin bottle in the cupboard over the sink, he shook a couple out into his hand, then filled a glass with cold water.

"Got a headache, huh?"

John downed the aspirin before answering his brother Mark, who had walked into the lunchroom and was pouring himself a cup of coffee.

"Yep. Been looking at numbers for too long, I guess. What are you doing back in town? I thought you were in Corpus all week."

"Finished the job early," Mark said. He sipped his coffee and eyed John over the rim of the cup. "You sure a headache's all that's wrong? You look a little down."

"I'm just tired."

Mark studied him thoughtfully.

John grimaced. "Oh, hell, I guess I *am* kind of depressed." He shrugged. "Next Wednesday would've been Cathy's and my fourteenth anniversary."

Mark grunted. "That's rough." His green eyes were filled with sympathy.

Suddenly John felt the need to be completely honest with his brother. "I'm okay. Really I am. I don't dwell on Cathy's death anymore. I—I guess the problem is I'm lonely . . . I've recently realized that I don't want to spend the rest of my life by myself." *And I can't get a certain blonde who lives across the street from me out of my mind. . . .*

"I've got just the solution," Mark said. "You need to get out more. Tell you what. We're having some friends over Saturday night. Why don't you come, too? I'll get Miranda to ask one of her single girlfriends. She's been wanting to try to fix you up for a while now, but I've been telling her I didn't think you were ready."

"No, I don't think—"

"I'm not taking no for an answer," Mark said. "You just admitted you're lonely. This'll be good for you."

"No, really, I don't want—"

"The party starts at seven. Dress is casual."

As in his earlier conversation with his son, John knew when he was beaten. "*Okay. I'll be there.*"

* * *

When Shelley got home Thursday night, Missy followed her into her bedroom while she changed her clothes. "Mom, our class is taking part in the city-wide Winter Science Project, and we really need another parent sponsor. I told Mrs. Bickham I'd ask you."

Shelley grimaced. She hated to refuse, but she was so busy right now. "Missy, I wish I could do it, but I just can't take off any more time from work than I'm already doing."

"It won't be during the day. It'll be at night."

Shelley carefully hung her suit jacket on a padded hanger. "Are you sure?" She unzipped her skirt.

"Yeah, I'm positive." Missy plopped on the bed and crossed her legs. "We'll be doin' some work on the project during school hours, but Mrs. Bickham will be there then. It's just at night and on Saturdays that the parents need to be there, 'cause we can't work unsupervised. If Dad lived here, I'd ask him...." Her voice trailed off sadly.

That's it, Missy, turn on the guilt.... "Well, I guess I c—"

"Oh, *thanks*, Mom!" All traces of her former sadness disappeared.

Shelley eyed her daughter thoughtfully. Had Missy purposely manipulated her into saying yes? Missy's expression was guileless, and Shelley immediately felt guilty for suspecting her of deviousness. "Do I need to call Mrs. Bickham or anything?"

"Uh-uh. I'll tell her."

"And then what?" Shelley hung her skirt on a skirt hanger and began unbuttoning her blouse.

"She'll pro'bly send you a note."

Shelley nodded and finished undressing while Missy filled her in on what had happened at school that day. Afterwards, they both headed for the kitchen where Shelley would start dinner and Missy would work on her homework.

Later that night, Shelley thought about her promise to Missy and decided it would probably be good for her to help out with the science project. It would get her out of the house a couple evenings a week, and she'd meet some of the other parents. Plus, this would be good, quality time with Missy. Once again, she thought about Missy's comment concerning Barry. Some of the anger she'd felt over that disastrous phone conversation the week of Missy's birthday returned. Since that day, there had been no communication from him. Shelley had half thought he might feel bad about what he'd said and send Missy a belated card or gift. But he hadn't, and Missy hadn't mentioned him until today.

Shelley pressed her lips together. Yes, she was doubly glad now she was going to be working with Missy and her class on this project. She wanted Missy to know that even though she only had one active, involved parent, that parent would always be there for her. Always.

What am I doing here? John thought. It was Saturday night, and he'd just arrived at Mark and Miranda's party. He'd never liked parties, especially ones where he didn't know many people. And now, single again after so many years of being part of a couple, he felt awkward and completely out of his depth. He had no idea how to act. He walked to the makeshift bar and mixed himself a scotch and water.

"C'mon, John, I'll introduce you around," Miranda said, walking up to him and smiling happily.

He couldn't help returning her smile, even though with each passing second, his desire to escape grew stronger. Miranda was one of the nicest people he'd ever known. She and Mark had been married for a little over two years, and they had just recently had their first baby—the cutest little girl. In addition to Miranda, her older sister, Clem, had married John's oldest brother, Luke, so now their families were really intertwined.

He followed Miranda around the room, nodding and smiling and trying to think of something interesting to say to her guests as she introduced them one by one. Finally she led him into the dining room where a tall brunette with very blue eyes behind black-framed, oversized glasses was standing talking to Molly, another of John's sisters-in-law, who was married to his brother Paul.

"Oh, *hi, John,*" Molly said brightly.

John didn't have to be hit over the head to know that the brunette was the woman invited especially for him.

Miranda introduced them. "This is Leigh Harrison. Leigh, my brother-in-law, John."

The brunette gave him a little, amused smile and extended her hand. "Nice to meet you, John." Her voice and body language were very self-assured and she met his gaze evenly.

For some reason, she made him nervous, but he hoped he didn't show it as he shook the proffered hand and returned her greeting. He felt like a green kid.

"Leigh's a psychologist," Molly chirped.

"That's nice," he murmured.

"We all met in Jazzercise class," Miranda volunteered.

He sipped at his scotch and nodded and wished he could think of something clever to say.

"John's an accountant," Molly added.

"Not really an accountant," he said. Hell, he hadn't even gone to college.

"Oh, he's so *modest*," Miranda interrupted. "Mark says he's a financial wizard. Say, why don't you two get acquainted, and Molly, how about coming into the kitchen and helping me with the food?"

Molly and Miranda, self-satisfied smiles on their faces, left. John wished he could leave, too, only he'd go straight out the back door.

"You're a widower, I understand," Leigh said. Her gaze was assessing.

"Yes." He wondered what else his well-intentioned sisters-in-law had told her about him.

"I've never been married."

John nodded. He had no idea what to say to her. He felt like an idiot. "Well," he finally managed, "marriage isn't for everyone."

"No, it's not."

Silence fell between them.

She broke it. "Miranda said you have two children."

John smiled in relief. Good. They could talk about his kids. He felt comfortable with that topic. "Yes. A girl, five, and a boy, eight."

"Nice ages. Old enough to do things for themselves and not so old that they think they know more than you do."

"Patrick, he's the eight-year-old, he's beginning to challenge me occasionally."

She took a sip of her wine and nodded. "How did they handle your wife's death?"

"Well, Nikki was awfully young when Cathy died, and after crying for her for a few days, she gradually stopped and seems to have adjusted well. Patrick, well, he's had a rougher time."

"Did you get counseling for them?"

John stiffened. What was she saying? That he *should* have gotten counseling for them? "No."

"Um." She eyed him over the rim of her glass.

"I would've gotten it for them if they'd needed it, but they didn't." Now, why was he explaining? He didn't owe her any explanations. He didn't even know this woman, and she certainly didn't know his children.

"Oh, I'm sure you're right." She smiled that little half-smile of hers again. "So, have you dated at all since your wife died?"

"No. Not much." *Not at all, unless you count the night I took Shelley to dinner.* Thinking of Shelley, John felt an acute stab of loneliness. God, he'd missed her the past couple of weeks! He had a sudden, nearly overwhelming need to talk to her and wished that instead of this shrewd-eyed, assessing woman standing next to him, Shelley were there with him. He laughed self-consciously. "It's kind of hard to start dating when you haven't done it for twenty years."

"Twenty years? Really? You don't look old enough to have been married that long."

"I wasn't. But Cathy and I started going together when we were juniors in high school."

Leigh Harrison nodded again.

John wondered what she was thinking behind those intimidating glasses. He felt miserably uncomfortable, as if she were judging him and finding him lacking. Whatever had possessed Miranda to think that he and this woman had anything in common? He took a swallow of his drink.

"Was she the only sexual partner you ever had?"

John choked on his drink. After coughing and finally catching his breath, he said, "Excuse me?"

There was that knowing smile again. "I think you heard the question," she said softly.

"I, uh . . ." He stopped, at a loss.

She shrugged. "I know. It's none of my business. I guess, as a psychologist, I'm just curious."

John was beginning to feel like a bug under a microscope. He cleared his throat. "Look, Miss Harrison—"

"Leigh."

"Leigh. I really don't want to discuss anything quite so personal. Do you mind?"

"I'll bet you're a wonderful lover."

John swallowed. He could feel his face growing hot. Jeez! Was this what it was like out there in the single world? He stared at Leigh Harrison. Was it his imagination, or did she resemble a black widow spider?

She moved in closer, and he could smell her musky perfume.

"If you like," she murmured, "we can leave early. I don't live very far away."

Her meaning was unmistakable. Suddenly, all John's nervousness and awkwardness fled.

"Thanks, Leigh," he said firmly. "I appreciate the offer, but I told my sitter I'd only be gone a couple of hours." He looked at his watch. "In fact, it's time I was heading home." He smiled. "It was a pleasure to meet you."

As he walked away, he knew without looking back that she still stood there, smiling that knowing smile.

What am I doing here? Shelley thought. She hadn't wanted to come to this party, but Linda had insisted upon dragging her along.

"You need *some* kind of social life," she'd said. "And Carolyn will be glad to have you."

So Shelley had asked Mrs. Dunbar to sit with Missy and she'd put on her black cocktail dress, and for the last two hours she'd been making small talk with people she didn't know and dancing with men who either held her too close or stepped on her feet and she'd even fended off one blatant pass where the guy had slid his hands down to cup her rear and she'd had to tell him to bug off... only she hadn't said *bug*.

The trouble was, she thought, staring down into her wineglass, that the whole dating/party scene was a real drag. She'd never enjoyed it in her pre-Barry days and she certainly didn't enjoy it now.

So why had she come?

You know why. You came because for the last two weeks, ever since John and the kids came for dinner that night, you've been feeling kind of low. And you've been thinking about him too much.

Even the good things that were in store for her on the job hadn't been able to dull the ache of loneliness that came over her every time she looked in the direction of John's house.

She sighed.

Yes, she guessed she'd thought it would be good for her to meet some other guys. Guys that would help her forget about John.

But this wasn't the way to do it. Coming here tonight had been a big mistake. Well, she didn't intend to keep compounding it. She was going home. Now.

The following Wednesday was the first night Shelley had to be at the school to help out with the class science project. "Is it okay if I wear jeans?" she asked Missy.

"Oh, sure, Mom."

So Shelley put on her favorite faded blue jeans, a well-worn sweatshirt and her sneakers and, along with Missy, headed for her school.

The first person Shelley saw when she entered Missy's classroom was John. Her heart leapt.

She could see by the expression in his eyes that he was just as surprised to see her as she was to see him. He was also pleased, if his smile was any indication.

"Did you get roped into becoming a parent sponsor, too?" he said, walking over to meet them. "Hi, Missy."

"Hi, Mr. Taylor." Missy left them and went over to join her classmates.

Although Shelley was flustered, she managed to inject just the right amount of amusement and exasperation into her voice. "Afraid so."

"It'll be fun," John said.

Shelley smiled. All she could think about were all the nights and Saturdays she would be in John's company.

Part of her was glad. Very glad.

The other part of her—the sensible part—knew this enforced togetherness was not a good idea.

In fact, it was completely and totally stupid.

If she had any sense at all, she'd call Mrs. Bickham tomorrow and make up some kind of excuse for why she had to back out.

"I've missed talking to you," John said.

Shelley's heart beat faster as she looked into his eyes. She swallowed. "I've missed . . . talking to you, too."

She knew then that she wasn't going to call Mrs. Bickham. After all, it wasn't that big a deal, was it? What was the worst that could happen?

You could get your silly heart broken, that's what.

As she smiled up at John, she thought that some chances were worth taking.

Chapter Nine

"So how have things been going at work the past couple of weeks?" John asked a little later that evening.

"Oh, great!" Shelley said happily, remembering that she hadn't had a chance to tell him about her talk with Walter Shaver. "In fact, the most wonderful thing happened."

She proceeded to recount her conversation with her boss and how he'd offered her the possibility of managing one of their future branch offices. "No one has ever shown that much confidence in my ability before," she confessed. "And I was thrilled. I'm *still* thrilled."

John seemed to hesitate before saying, "That's terrific, Shelley. He must think a lot of you."

Was it Shelley's imagination, or did John seem less than one hundred percent enthusiastic about her news? Shelley tried to swallow her doubts, but she couldn't help feeling that John didn't approve of what she'd told him. What did that mean? That he thought she shouldn't take on a job like that? Or worse, that he thought maybe she couldn't handle it? Or that she'd be neglecting Missy if she took it? The last thought hurt.

"This means a lot to me, you know," she finally said. "It will give me a lot more security because I won't be relying strictly on commissions. As a manager of one of the branch offices, I would get a salary and benefits. I'd be an employee of the agency rather than an independent contractor who has to purchase her own medical insurance and life insurance and pay her own social security."

"Oh. I hadn't thought of all that."

"No, I didn't think you had."

He smiled a bit sheepishly. "I'm really glad for you, Shelley. You've worked hard, and you deserve this."

His words made her feel better, but she still cautioned herself not to count on too much from John. Although he'd come a long way from his original disapproval of her, and she thought of him as a real friend now, he obviously still had reservations about the way she was living her life and some of the choices she made.

She told herself yet again that it would be sheer folly to fall in love with him. *He'll end up hurting you— you'd better remember that....*

For the rest of the evening, she felt a sense of disquiet and she knew he felt it, too, because she caught him looking at her several times, and his expression was subdued and thoughtful. When nine o'clock came, and it was time to clean up and leave for the night, she even thought he was going to say something about their earlier conversation, but all he said was, "We'll walk out to the parking lot with you."

"Thanks."

"You know," he said when they reached her car, "since we're both helping out with this project, why don't we all just ride to the school together? No sense in having two cars here."

"That's probably true."

He nodded. "Keep me posted about that manager's position."

"I will, but nothing's going to happen for a while. They haven't even started looking for office space yet." She unlocked her car door.

"I really hope you get it. You know that, don't you?" he said quietly.

"Sure. I know that."

"If I gave you any other impression, I'm sorry."

"Hey, no problem," she said. "Don't worry about it."

He smiled. "Well, good night." He bent down to look into the car. "Good night, Missy."

"Good night, Mr. Taylor," Missy said.

Then Shelley climbed into her car and shut the door. As she pulled out of the parking lot, she could see Patrick and John walking toward their car. For some reason, the two figures seemed lonely, and she thought how nice it would have been to be driving home together, like a family.

But you're not a family, and you never will be.

Shelley sighed, told herself to quit wishing for things she couldn't have, and pointed her car toward home.

John told himself not to get too attached to Shelley or too used to being with her. But over the next weeks, it was sometimes hard to remember his admonition.

He was spending more and more time in her company. Even if he'd wanted to pull back, it seemed every time he turned around, Patrick was saying, "We need to work on our project tonight, Dad. We're gettin' behind."

"This is taking a lot more time than you said it would, Patrick," John complained, but he didn't really mind. He enjoyed being with Shelley and the kids, even as he told himself it wasn't wise to get too used to having her around. One Sunday afternoon in early November, when Shelley and John had been helping with the science project for almost three weeks, Shelley said, "You know what they're doing, don't you?"

"Who?" he answered, smiling. "The kids?"

"Yes, the kids."

"No. What are they doing?"

She grinned. "You mean you really don't know?"

"Know *what?*"

She laughed. "They're trying to matchmake. That's why they keep maneuvering us into all these extra meetings."

John stared, flabbergasted. Of course. He couldn't believe that he hadn't realized it long before now. So many things became clear to him.

Her amusement was tinged with self-consciousness as she watched him assimilate what she'd said. "I hope you don't mind. I just thought you needed to know."

He shook his head, chuckling. "Do you believe those kids? Hell, they're as bad as my sisters-in-law...." The memory of the fiasco with Leigh Harrison returned, and he mentally shuddered. At least the kids had more sense about the type of woman he'd be interested in. The thought floored him. Here he'd been telling himself for months that Shelley was not his type, and in many ways she had turned out to be very much his type. If only they wanted the same things out of life...

"I have a feeling this whole thing might be Missy's idea," Shelley said, breaking into his thoughts. "She... well..." She shrugged. "Missy wants a father, and she's crazy about you."

John glanced over at the little girl, who sat giggling with Patrick at the dining room table where they were supposed to be lettering signs for the different stages in the development of the sewing machine, which was their particular part of the project. Something tugged at his heart.

"I'm sorry, John, if this makes you uncomfortable."

"No, don't be sorry! I'm, well, if you want to know the truth, I'm touched. Missy's a wonderful kid. I'd be proud to be her father."

Their gazes clung for a long moment. "You're a very nice man, John, you know that, don't you?" Her voice and eyes were soft.

Suddenly, all John's good resolutions flew out the window. He desperately wished they were alone. He desperately wished the kids weren't in the next room and Froggie wasn't upstairs. He wished this because he wanted, more than anything, to pull Shelley into his arms and kiss her thoroughly. He wanted this so badly it was nearly a physical pain.

He saw her swallow, saw the awareness slide into her eyes, and knew that she knew what he was feeling. The seconds ticked away. He cleared his throat. "Did you, uh, did you have any ideas about how we might handle this whole thing?"

"Well, I don't think we really need to do anything. I just wanted you to know what I suspected, and that way, we can kind of counter anything that's unwelcome. . . ." She looked down so he could no longer see her eyes. "And let them down gently, of course."

"Of course." Her suggestion was completely sensible. In fact, it was the only way to handle the situation. Despite knowing this, disappointment stabbed him.

For the rest of the evening, he continued to think about what Shelley had told him and the conclusion they'd reached.

We'll let them down gently.

He told himself that he wouldn't have wanted it any other way. He certainly wouldn't want to lead the kids on or give them any hope that their plan was working. What would be the point in that?

He reluctantly concluded that the sooner the work on the science project was over, the better for all concerned.

The science project neared completion the second week of November, just about the time the weather cooled off and the trees began to turn.

The kids would probably finish their portion of the project the following afternoon. They had done all their research on the sewing machine and were almost finished building the model of the original invention. That, coupled with a portable sewing machine of today, and the drawings of the different stages of development through the years, represented their contribution.

Shelley was relieved. It was all for the best that her involvement was nearly over she told herself, while driving home from work that Friday night. If she'd ever had any doubts, John's reaction to her news about the possible manager's job had shown her, once and for all, that he would never wholly approve of her. Which meant she would never allow herself to become involved with him.

If and when Shelley had another serious, romantic relationship, it would be with a man who thought she was wonderful in every way, a man who backed her totally, and most important, a man who would not constantly be comparing her to some other, loftier ideal where Shelley was bound to always come up short, the way she had in her relationships with her parents and her ex-husband.

She cast a regretful glance in the direction of John's house as she swung into her driveway. *Too bad. It's really too bad....*

"You're home early," Mrs. Dunbar said when Shelley walked inside.

"Yes. The closing didn't last as long as I'd expected it to." Shelley took off her raincoat—it had been raining when she'd left for work that morning—and hung it on the clothes tree in the hall.

"Well, good," the older woman said, "because there's something I need to talk to you about."

Something about her tone alerted Shelley to the fact that she probably wasn't going to like whatever it was Mrs. Dunbar had on her mind. Still, she had no premonition of what the woman was going to say, so when she said it, a few minutes later, Shelley's heart sank.

"Y-you're quitting?"

"I'm sorry, Shelley, I really am. I hate to be doing this to you, but I've made up my mind. I want to be closer to Nancy. I'm moving to San Diego by the end of the month."

Nancy was Mrs. Dunbar's only child, and she and her husband and their two little boys had moved to San Diego a year earlier. Shelley knew the older woman missed her grandchildren desperately.

"I'm sorry, too," Shelley said, "but I understand."

But what was she going to do for a sitter for Missy? Shelley had interviewed dozens of potential sitters before finally finding Mrs. Dunbar. It wasn't easy to get someone not only reliable, but trustworthy and honest and likable, who really liked children. Not to mention someone Shelley could afford.

"I didn't tell Missy," Mrs. Dunbar said.

"That's okay. I'd rather tell her myself."

That night, after Shelley and Missy had finished their dinner and they were cleaning up the kitchen, Shelley broke the news.

Missy's face fell. "But I don't want Mrs. Dunbar to go."

"I know. I don't, either."

"I'm gonna miss her."

"I know you are, sweetie. So am I." Shelley finished scrubbing the casserole dish and put it in the dish drainer and thought about how the people Missy loved always seemed to be abandoning her. "You know, don't you, that Mrs. Dunbar really cares for you and hates to leave you?"

"Then why is she?"

Shelley stopped what she was doing and turned to face Missy. "Honey, listen, when you grow up and maybe get married, if you had to move away, wouldn't you miss me a lot? Wouldn't you want me to be there?"

Missy looked down. "Yeah," she said reluctantly.

"Well," Shelley said gently, "that's the way it is with Mrs. Dunbar and Nancy. Nancy's Mrs. Dunbar's daughter, just like you're my daughter, and they miss each other."

Missy nodded.

"I'm sorry, honey."

Missy finally looked up. "But who's gonna baby-sit me?" She took the casserole dish out of the drainer and began to dry it.

Shelley sighed. "I don't know. I'll talk to some people. Ask around. Maybe advertise. We'll figure out something."

For the rest of the evening, Shelley thought about the situation. After awhile, she had an idea. Later, when she was sitting on the edge of Missy's bed in preparation for saying good-night, she decided to test the waters. "You know, honey, I've been thinking. How about, instead of me trying to find another sitter to come to the house, we enroll you in an after-school program at one of the day-care centers?"

Missy sat up in alarm. "No, Mom, I don't want to go to a day-care center! That's for little kids."

"No, it isn't, sweetie. In fact, lots of kids your age get picked up at school and go to day care. It would probably be fun for you."

"No, it wouldn't! If I had to go someplace like that, I wouldn't be able to play with Patrick anymore." Missy's face crumpled and she looked as if she were going to burst into tears at any moment. "I don't *wanna* go to a day-care center. I wanna stay here, just like I always have. I don't need a baby-sitter. I can stay by myself."

"Missy, you can't stay by yourself. Why, the few times you've had to, you've hated it. You were scared."

"I know, but I'm eight now, and I'm not scared anymore."

"Oh, Missy..."

"I'm not, Mom. I'm not! Promise me you won't make me go to a day care. Promise me!"

Shelley could see Missy was becoming hysterical. "Okay, okay, honey, now shush," she said soothingly. "Don't worry. We'll think of something else."

"But do you promise?"

"Yes, yes, I promise."

She finally got Missy settled down again and leaned over to kiss her cheek. "'Night, sweetie."

"'Night, Mom."

Shelley turned out Missy's light and slowly walked back to the living room. She hoped with all her heart that she hadn't made Missy a promise she couldn't keep.

* * *

"Why so glum, Missy?" John said the following morning.

"My baby-sitter quit, and my mom's worried 'cause she's afraid she won't be able to find someone else."

"Yeah, Dad, and maybe Missy might have to go to a *day-care* center!" Patrick said.

"Would that be so bad?" John asked.

"Dad!" Patrick said. "If Missy's in a day-care center, we can't play together after school."

"I'd *hate* going to a center," Missy said.

"Yeah, she'd *hate* it!" Patrick echoed.

"Ahh. Now I understand," John said.

Later that afternoon, when John and Shelley were at the school for the last session on the science project, he finally got a chance to ask about her dilemma.

"Yes," she said, grimacing. "I don't know what I'm going to do."

"How long do you have?"

"Mrs. Dunbar gave me two weeks' notice."

"Not very long."

"No."

"What if you haven't found someone suitable by the time she's ready to go?"

Shelley glanced over at the kids, then lowered her voice. "I don't know. Despite my promise to Missy, I think I have to investigate some of the day-care centers. I might be forced to fall back on one, and I've got to be prepared." She shot Missy another look. "I understand how she feels, but there are some wonderful centers around, and I think she'd adjust quickly." Her face was a picture of consternation.

That night John kept thinking about Shelley's problem. He was still thinking about it the following morning. After they all got home from church, he mentioned the situation to Froggie.

"I don't know what the solution is," he said. "She has to work." Of course, Shelley liked working, but he didn't add that. Whether she liked working or not, the fact remained that she had to support herself and her child. And that meant she needed good, reliable day care.

Froggie studied him thoughtfully for a long moment. "John, how would you feel about *me* watching Missy?"

"You?"

"Yes. She's over here half the time, anyway, or Patrick is over there. Why not? Missy's no trouble at all, and I'd be happy to help Shelley out."

"She'd pay you, of course," John said thoughtfully. He examined the idea of Froggie keeping Missy. And the more he thought about it, the more he liked it. It really was the perfect solution. "Are you sure you want to? Don't say you do if you have any doubts."

Froggie smiled. "I don't have any doubts. I'm here, anyway. What's one more child, especially one as sweet and well-behaved as Missy?"

That evening, after John and the kids got home from Sunday dinner at his mother's, he decided to walk over to Shelley's and tell her about Froggie's offer.

"You go ahead," Froggie said. "I'll give Nikki her bath while you're gone."

He walked across the street and rang Shelley's doorbell.

"John!" she said when she opened the door. Her eyes lit up in welcome. "Hi! Come on in. What brings you here?"

He walked inside and looked around. "Where's Missy?"

"She's in her room. Why? Did you want to see her?"

"No, I wanted to talk to you, but I didn't want her to overhear."

"Oh. Well, let's go back to the kitchen, then." Her eyes were curious.

"Okay."

When they reached the kitchen, she asked him if he wanted something to drink. "Coffee? A beer? Or a soft drink?"

He looked at the coffeemaker and saw that there was still some in the pot. "I'll have some coffee."

Once they were seated, he said, "I talked to Froggie about Mrs. Dunbar quitting."

Shelley nodded.

John could tell from her expression that she had no idea what was coming. "Froggie wondered how you'd feel about her watching Missy."

Shelley stared at him. "John! Do you mean it? Froggie? Froggie offered to watch Missy, too?"

He smiled. "Yes."

"And you don't mind? You approve?"

His smile turned quizzical. "Why would I mind?"

Shelley swallowed. "Oh, John . . ." Her eyes filled with tears. "I—I don't know what to say."

"Hey," he said softly.

She got up and walked over to the counter where there was a box of facial tissue. With her back to him, she blew her nose.

John stood. He walked over to her and touched her shoulder. "Shelley..."

She turned. Their eyes met.

And then suddenly she was in his arms, and he was kissing her.

Once.

Twice.

Three times.

With each kiss, his heart thundered harder. With each kiss the desire he'd tamped down for so long flared into heated life, racing through him like a fire races through a tinder-dry forest, igniting everything in its path. With each kiss, his common sense got weaker and his need got stronger.

It had been such a long time.

And he wanted this woman so much.

He crushed her to him, everything else forgotten: where they were, the fact that Missy was home, the fact that he was doing something impulsively—something he'd probably regret tomorrow.

"John, John, we can't do this...Missy's home...." Shelley's urgent whisper finally penetrated the heat of desire consuming him.

He slowly and reluctantly released her, his emotions tumultuous. He looked down at her. Her lips looked swollen and her face was flushed.

"God, Shelley, I'm sorry. I don't know what happened."

She swallowed, looking away. "I—I think you'd better go."

"Yes." He felt like kicking himself. Damn! What was wrong with him? "We—we'll talk tomorrow, okay?"

She nodded, still not meeting his eyes.

"I'll call you at the office in the morning. Maybe we can have lunch together."

Finally she looked up. "Okay."

He wanted to say something else, but he knew he'd better hightail it out of there. Best to sleep on this and think it through before he said another word.

Chapter Ten

John hadn't been out the door five minutes when Shelley's mother called.

"Your father and I are coming to visit this weekend," she announced.

Shelley groaned inwardly—just what she needed, a visit from her parents—but she managed to sound enthusiastic. "That's great, Mom. How long are you planning to stay?"

"I don't know, Shelley. That depends on how things go," Vivian Cochrane answered, her voice sliding into the icy tone Shelley knew so well.

Gee, Mom, why are you bothering? Shelley thought resentfully. She couldn't help it. She knew she should be glad to see her parents because she saw them so seldom, and after all, they *were* her parents. But they always acted as if visiting her was a distasteful duty they felt compelled to fulfill but didn't enjoy at all, and they always made her feel as if they were silently criticizing her every word and action.

"I just wondered if I should arrange for some vacation," she said. "I thought, if you were planning to stay over into next week, that I'd take Monday and Tuesday off."

"Well, I'm sorry, but I don't know," her mother repeated. "We'll see how your father is feeling."

Shelley rolled her eyes. Her mother always used her father as an excuse when she didn't want to be pinned down or when she wanted to get out of something. "Okay. No problem."

"We'll probably get there about six on Friday. We'll be tired, so we'd prefer to eat dinner in."

This was a not-so-subtle reminder that Shelley had taken them out to eat on their first night in town during their last visit—an excursion that ended in disaster when something her mother ate disagreed with her and she was up all night.

"Don't worry, we'll eat in."

"And no shrimp. Your father's allergic to it."

"Yes, Mother, I know."

"And no red meat."

"I know that, too."

"Just do chicken on the grill or something. We're not picky. We don't need fancy food."

No, you're not picky, and Houston's not hot in August.

"Or fish . . . some kind of fish would be nice," her mother continued.

"Okay, great. Listen, I've gotta go. I have another call coming in." Which was a lie, but her mother wouldn't know it.

Shelley knew she wouldn't be able to go to sleep that night, and she was right. She lay there, her thoughts tumbling around in her head like balls in a wire lottery cage.

Her thoughts ricocheted between the call from her mother and the episode with John. Finally, she willed herself to stop thinking about the impending visit from her parents. There was no sense in continuing to worry about it—she would get through it. It might not be much fun, but at least it wouldn't last forever.

John was another story.

She was enormously grateful to him. His offer of Froggie as a solution to Shelley's baby-sitting problem was the answer to a prayer. Shelley hadn't yet told Missy and knew that when her daughter found out she would be going to Patrick's house every day, she would be thrilled. And Shelley was thrilled that John was in favor of the arrangement.

No. Froggie baby-sitting wasn't the problem. What *was* a problem and the thing that was keeping her awake, emotions churning crazily, was what had happened between her and John right before he left.

She still couldn't figure out how she had ended up in his arms. Oh, God! It was bad enough that she'd kissed him with Missy right in the next room, but the *way* she'd kissed him! As if he were a five-course meal and she was a starving woman....

Her face flamed each time she thought about her response to him. What must he think?

What's wrong with you? she asked herself again and again. *Don't you have any sense? Don't you have any self-control? What the hell did you think you were doing? Missy could've walked in on you at any moment, and then what?*

Even though the situation wasn't funny, Shelley couldn't help a silent chuckle at the thought of Missy walking into the kitchen and seeing them, because if Missy *had* caught them kissing, she would probably have been delighted.

Yeah, Shelley told herself wryly, *she'd have been planning the wedding....*

Thank goodness John had suggested they talk about their relationship, because it was obvious they needed to. She wondered what he would say. She was afraid he was going to say he was sorry, and she wasn't sure she could handle that.

What do you want him to say? That he's in love with you? That's not going to happen. And do you really want it to?

Shelley squeezed her eyes shut. Oh, God, she didn't know what she wanted. She only hoped, when she and John talked the next day, that she wouldn't make a fool of herself or say something she'd regret.

Shelley was afraid to leave the office the next morning because she didn't want to miss John's call. She kept looking at the clock and hoping he'd call early.

She was thankful she didn't have to wait too long. His call came through a few minutes past nine-thirty.

"Do you still want to meet me for lunch?" he said.

"Yes," she answered as casually as she could manage over her skidding heartbeat.

"Name the place."

She'd already decided on a place. She hadn't wanted to run into anyone from the office, so she'd chosen somewhere that wasn't too close. "How about The Mason Jar on the Katy Freeway?"

"That sounds good. What time?"

"How about eleven-thirty?"

"All right. I'll see you then."

When she hung up, her heart was still racing, and she told herself to calm down. She was acting like a goofy kid. But she couldn't help it. She was excited and nervous and half anxiously awaiting, half dreading the meeting.

She kept looking at the clock. The hands were moving more slowly than they'd ever moved before.

Finally it was time to go. Shelley timed it so that at precisely 11:29 she was pulling into the restaurant's parking lot. She was pleased to see that John was already there, waiting for her outside the front door. He smiled when he saw her approaching.

Shelley's pulse rate accelerated despite her stern admonition to stay cool. He looked so handsome in his dark suit paired with a pale yellow shirt and charcoal geometric print tie—so completely masculine and sexy. Both his eyes and his dark hair gleamed in the sunlight. He looked as if he'd dressed with care, as if he were meeting an important customer, which made Shelley feel good.

She had dressed carefully that morning, too. She was wearing her newest addition to her career wardrobe—a soft wool suit in forest green, paired with a pale blue silk blouse. She'd even found some big diamond-shaped earrings studded with tiny blue and green stones that were the perfect accessory for her outfit. She knew the colors complemented her hair and eyes and the earrings made her look feminine and sophisticated. She'd taken special care with her makeup, too, wanting to look her very best.

John's admiring gaze told her she'd succeeded on all counts.

"Hi," he said. "You look nice."

"Thanks. You do, too."

They smiled at each other, and Shelley's stomach got that hollowed-out feeling that it always got when she was nervous and excited.

They didn't talk as they were ushered into the restaurant and seated. Even then, their conversation was limited to comments on how nice the weather was and how crowded the restaurant was already. Shelley told herself to relax.

Their waitress came and took their drink orders. After she left, John said, "I, uh, thought maybe we could save our discussion for after lunch."

"After lunch?"

"Yeah, there's a little park near my office. Hardly anyone goes there during the week, and I thought we might just drive over there and sit on a bench and talk...in private."

"All right," Shelley said reluctantly. Although she saw the wisdom of waiting until they had some privacy, she didn't know if she could get through an entire lunch without betraying how nervous she was.

Somehow she did.

Somehow she ate her baked potato soup and salad and John ate his baked potato soup and half a sandwich, and they discussed innocuous subjects and Shelley got through it without spilling anything or doing anything to embarrass herself.

Forty-five minutes later, John paid the bill, leaving a generous tip, Shelley noticed, and with a great sense of relief mixed with trepidation, she preceded him out of the restaurant.

"Do you want to ride over to the park with me, then I'll bring you back here?" John offered.

"No, I'll just follow you." Much better that way, she thought. If she had her own car, she could make a quick getaway if she needed to.

The little park was located right off Memorial Drive within two blocks of John's office, which they passed on their way. As John had promised, it was small and pleasant and secluded. Shelley parked next to John in the tiny parking lot, which she figured probably held eight cars maximum.

"This is really nice," she said, looking around. The park was maybe an acre of wooded land smack-dab in the middle of a subdivision, but John assured her it was a public area. There were half a dozen wooden benches placed in a loose circle around a central flower garden planted with a profusion of chrysanthemums and other late-season blooms in a variety of colors. Big oak and pine trees shaded the area, and the walkways were paved in a springy black substance that was softer than concrete and just right for roller blading, biking or strolling.

Only one other person was there—an older woman dressed in sweats and sneakers—obviously cooling down after a noonday run. She smiled at them as they passed her and they nodded and smiled back.

They sat on the bench farthest from the entrance. A blue jay squawked at them and flew off noisily; they'd obviously routed it from a favorite spot.

Shelley chuckled. "I love jays. They're so opinion-ated. You always know where you stand with them." Immediately she wondered if John would take her re-mark as a double entendre. She took a deep breath. God, this might even be harder than she'd imagined.

John brushed off the bench with a handkerchief. He smiled at her. "I think it's clean."

They sat.

For a moment, neither said anything. The sights and sounds of the November day filled the air: birds call-ing to each other from the depths of the trees, the sunlight making dappled patterns on the grass, cars humming on the macadam beyond, a bee busily working the flower garden, and somewhere high overhead the distant whine of a jet winging its way north through the crystal blue sky.

Shelley took a deep breath of the clean, cool air. She looked at John. His eyes met hers—an irresistible combination of brown, green, and gold that always did something to her heart when she looked into them.

He reached for her hand.

Excitement rippled through her at his touch.

"Shelley," he said softly, "after last night, I think you know that I want you."

Her heart leapt crazily. She swallowed, hard. "I—I'm not sure what to say."

"I think you feel the same way."

She hadn't been prepared for such directness. She wished she were more experienced, more sophisticated, more used to dealing with situations like this.

"Was I wrong?" he pressed.

She decided it was only fair to be as honest with him as he was being with her. She wet her lips. *Come on, don't be such a chicken, say it!* "No. You weren't wrong. I—I want you, too."

He squeezed her hand. "But I don't think either one of us can afford to leap into a relationship, especially a physical one, casually."

"Oh, I absolutely agree," she said quickly. Now that their feelings were out in the open, she felt calmer. "For one thing, there're the children. I won't ever do anything that might hurt Missy... or your children."

"Good. I feel the same way."

"And..." Her eyes met his again. "Quite honestly, John, I'm not sure I can handle this right now."

He nodded thoughtfully.

"See, the thing is, I'm dealing with a lot of pressure on my job...but that's not all." She sighed. "Last night after you left, my mother called and said she and my father are coming to visit this weekend, and, well, a visit from them is always stressful."

"So are you saying you think we should just try to forget about how we feel?"

"Isn't that what you were saying?" she hedged.

"That's probably the sensible thing to do," he said slowly.

She nodded. "Yes." She was proud of herself. She didn't betray how much that answer had cost her.

"The trouble is, I'm not sure I can do that." His gaze captured hers.

Something curled deep in Shelley's stomach. "I—I'm not sure I can, either," she said honestly. "But don't you think we should just . . . think about everything for a few days? You know, kind of put things on hold? Just until my parents are gone, anyway? And then . . . well, maybe we can talk some more and . . . see how we feel."

His smile was slow and sweet and intensified that aching hunger that had begun the first time he'd kissed her. "I think that's a good plan."

Shelley wished he'd quit looking at her mouth. She knew he wanted to kiss her. She also knew she'd done the right thing in asking for more time. She just couldn't afford to do anything so serious without thinking it through thoroughly and unemotionally. It was too important. The ramifications were too serious.

"How long are your parents staying?" he asked, finally releasing her hand.

"I don't know. I asked, but my mother said they'd wait and see how things go."

He frowned. "How things go?"

"Yeah, as in, *if we're getting along and if you're being a good girl and doing everything right, maybe we'll stay past the weekend.* You know." She tried to keep her voice from sounding bitter. But it was hard.

She could see by his expression that he didn't understand, but she didn't have the energy to explain that her mother—and her father, although not quite to the extent of her mother—would spend every minute in silent and not-so-silent criticism of her. They would find fault with everything. The way the house looked. The way she looked. The way Missy looked. The food she served them. The weather. You name it, they wouldn't like something about it. And eventually, even though she'd told herself not to, Shelley would get defensive and angry and she would answer her parents in shorter and more sarcastic sentences.

And then, inevitably, the way it always did, their visit would end with strained feelings all around.

"Let's not talk about them, okay?" she said, looking at her watch and seeing that it was one o'clock. "I think I'd better be getting back to work."

"Yes, I guess I should, too."

They got up and walked back to the parking area. When they reached her car, Shelley slowly turned to face John. She felt suddenly self-conscious and uncertain. There were so many emotions welling within.

He looked down at her for a long moment. Then, before she could react or resist, before she could even think whether she wanted him to or not, he tipped her chin up and kissed her.

His lips were warm as they settled against hers. Shelley's pulse fluttered wildly. The kiss didn't last a long time as kisses went, but it packed an emotional punch that left her feeling light-headed when it was over.

"I'm sorry. I couldn't resist," John murmured, smiling slightly as he released her. He touched his forefinger to the tip of her nose. "I'll call you. Okay?"

"Okay."

Well, girl, now you've gone and done it, Shelley thought as she pulled out of the parking lot. *After telling yourself not to, after telling yourself you're not ready, and especially after telling yourself that you*

*want a man who approves of you one hundred per-
cent—you've fallen in love with John, anyway.*

"Something on your mind?" Froggie said that night
after the kids had gone up to bed.

John blinked. "Sorry. What did you say?"

"I just wondered if something was bothering you.
You've been awfully quiet all night."

John lowered the magazine that he'd been staring at
for the past hour without comprehending a word.
"No. I was just . . . thinking."

"You sure? You seem terribly preoccupied."

"I'm sure."

Froggie nodded and turned her attention back to the
television program she'd been watching, but her eyes
had remained speculative, and John knew he hadn't
convinced her.

He wondered what her reaction would be if she
knew what he *had* been thinking about. Ever since
he'd said goodbye to Shelley after their talk in the
park—no, ever since he'd *kissed* Shelley goodbye in
the park—he hadn't been able to think about anything else.

He knew it would be better if he didn't start this
kind of relationship with Shelley. He had kept telling
himself this all last night and all day today.

Too late. You've already started it.

It was too late. He not only desired her, he was
emotionally entangled with her.

The only question left was, where would they go
from here?

* * *

Shelley tried to put all thoughts of John out of her mind as she readied the house and herself for the arrival of her parents on Friday night. She cleaned the house until it shone, polishing furniture, washing dishes and the few pieces of crystal that were a legacy from her marriage, vacuuming, dusting. She even took down the kitchen curtains and washed and ironed them.

She brushed the cats, she watered her plants and sprayed the leaves, she washed all the windows, she changed the sheets in the guest room, she scrubbed the guest bath to within an inch of its life, and she made sure she had plenty of diet drinks, without caffeine, for her mother and a supply of root beer and Bailey's Irish Cream for her father.

On Friday afternoon, she left work at three and stopped by Randalls, picking up freshly baked French bread, romaine lettuce, tomatoes, mushrooms, carrots, and green onions for a salad, broccoli for a casserole, and already-stuffed flounder fillets from the meat department. Then she splurged on a bouquet of flowers from the floral department and a lemon-chess pie from the bakery.

She grimaced, thinking she'd blown several days' food budget on her purchases. But it couldn't be helped. She could no more stop herself from trying to please and impress her parents than she could stop breathing.

She glanced over at John's house when she got home. The garage was open, but only Froggie's little red Toyota was in the garage. John was still at work.

Shelley wondered what John would think of her parents, whether he would understand how they made her feel or if he would think she was overreacting, making more of their behavior than it warranted. Well, she wasn't going to find out what he thought—not on this visit, anyway—because she had no intention of introducing him to her parents this weekend.

But she had a feeling John was curious and that he'd been hoping she would suggest an introduction. She thought back to their conversation Wednesday night, when he had called her as promised.

"If there's anything you need . . ." he'd said, referring to her preparations for the upcoming visit.

"Thanks, but I'm fine," she'd said firmly.

"Have you decided what you're going to do while your parents are here?"

"Yes. On Saturday I'm taking them shopping. That's the one thing about Houston my mother actually likes. The shopping is a lot better than what she has at home. And Saturday night we've been invited to have dinner at my friend Linda's house, and Sunday we'll go to church and then to brunch."

He was silent for a moment, then said, "So you'll be around the rest of the day?"

It was then Shelley realized what he was hinting at. For a fraction of a second, she considered suggesting he come over to meet them, but she knew she couldn't handle it. She knew she was at far less than her best when in the company of her parents' silent disapproval, and she didn't want John to see her that way. If they were married, it would be different—but they weren't. "I don't know if we will or not," she hedged.

"Dad might want to watch football, and maybe my mother and Missy and I will go out. It depends."

John didn't press the matter, and Shelley was grateful. They'd hung up with him saying, "Enjoy their visit."

Yeah, sure, Shelley thought now as she unloaded her groceries. *Like an IRS audit!*

When Missy arrived home after her gymnastics lesson, Shelley already had the dining room table set, her salad made and in the refrigerator, her broccoli, cheese and rice casserole bubbling in the oven, and the fillets laid out in a shallow dish and ready for baking.

"Take all your things to your room, hon, then wash your face and hands and change into that new blue dress of yours, okay?" she said to Missy.

"Okay. What time are Grandma and Grandpa coming?" Missy said.

"They should be here in less than an hour." Shelley's stomach clenched. She closed her eyes and counted slowly to twenty. *I will not get nervous. I will not get upset. These are just my parents, not ogres.*

At three minutes after six, Shelley heard the car pulling into the driveway. She wiped her hands on her apron, then noticed it was stained and yanked it off, tossing it into the laundry room. She smoothed her hair back, took a deep breath, summoned the most enthusiastic smile she could manage, and said brightly, "They're here, Missy."

A grinning Missy ran ahead. By the time Shelley reached the front door, her parents were already out of their Buick and her father had the trunk open and was removing their bags. He looked up as Shelley walked outside. He smiled and waved and Shelley waved back.

Missy stood talking to her grandmother. Vivian glanced up as Shelley approached. Her eyes, cool and pale blue, made an assessing sweep, and Shelley knew her mother had taken in the black stirrup pants, the oversized white sweater, the black loafers, Shelley's makeup and Shelley's hairstyle, all in that one encompassing look. Shelley also knew her mother had probably found something wrong with most of it.

"Hello, dear," her mother said.

"Hi, Mom. Did you have a good trip?"

"As good as can be expected."

Shelley nodded.

They hugged. Her mother's body felt rigid and ungiving. Shelley wondered why it was always like this between them. She wondered if there was any way to change things but knew there wasn't. Hadn't she been trying all of her life?

Shelley walked over and hugged her father, and his greeting was warmer—he gave her a light kiss on the cheek—but it wasn't exuberant, because he was a naturally undemonstrative man. Besides, Shelley knew that he was very much aware that his wife would not approve of an effusive greeting, and Richard Cochrane had obviously decided long ago to please his wife above all others, even if his daughter suffered as a consequence.

Shelley shook off her momentary twinge of disappointment, telling herself she was a ninny to have expected anything to be different. *They'll never change. Quit thinking they will. . . .*

The four of them walked into the house, Shelley studying her parents surreptitiously to see if there were any physical changes since she'd last seen them fifteen months earlier. Her mother hadn't changed at all, she decided. Still trim and attractive at sixty-three, Vivian Cochrane walked ramrod straight and retained the same figure she'd had in her twenties. The only hint that she was aging were the crow's-feet around her eyes and the grooves beginning to show at the corners of her mouth. As usual, her mother was faultlessly dressed in dark blue gabardine slacks and matching sweater.

At sixty-nine, Shelley's father was starting to really show his age and seemed a little more stooped than he had before. He was a tall man, slightly balding, with dark eyes and a narrow face and long, thin nose.

Shelley had inherited her height from her father, her blond hair and coloring from her mother.

Her father started to set down the bags in the foyer, but Shelley's mother said, "Put the bags in the guest room, Richard," and he immediately headed for the bedroom wing.

"Honestly," her mother said, "you'd think he'd know better by now." She walked into the living room and looked around. "I see you've still got that old blue sofa. Did I tell you that Suzanne recently redid her living room? You should see it. It's really a showplace. Of course, she inherited my good taste."

Shelley gritted her teeth.

She was afraid it was going to be one hell of a long weekend.

Chapter Eleven

All weekend John found himself making excuses to be outside. He raked leaves on Saturday, dragging the chore out as long as he could, and his patience was rewarded. About one o'clock, Missy, Shelley and Shelley's parents came outside and headed for the Buick. He waved, and Shelley waved back, but she didn't walk over with her parents or make any other indication that she'd like him to meet them.

Her mother had given him a curious look before getting into the car, and John had a brief impression of an attractive, slender woman with blond hair. The only thing John could tell about Shelley's father was that he was tall and thin.

On Sunday afternoon, John made an excuse to leave the ritual Sunday dinner and afternoon visit at his mother's house early, saying he had some work to do around the house. At four, when he and the kids arrived home, he saw that both Shelley's and her parents' cars were in her driveway.

At five he could no longer contain his curiosity. "Hey, Froggie," he said, poking his head into the kitchen where Froggie was putting together a casserole of macaroni and cheese. "I'm going across the street to Shelley's for a minute, okay?"

Froggie gave him an enigmatic look. "You do know her parents are visiting this weekend, don't you?"

"Yes, I know."

"Curious about them, are you?"

He laughed. "You see right through me, Froggie."

"So what reason are you using for your visit?"

"I don't know. I guess I hadn't thought that far ahead. Got any suggestions?"

Froggie grinned. "Sure. Tell her I sent you over to borrow a cup of sugar."

Five minutes later, as John rang Shelley's doorbell, he wondered if she would see through his ploy.

Her eyes rounded when she answered the door and saw him standing there. "John! What?" She stopped, obviously flustered to see him. She cleared her throat. "Um, what brings you here?"

He gave her a sheepish look. "Froggie sent me over to borrow a cup of sugar."

"Oh. Well, uh, would you like to come in?"

"Thanks." He stepped into the house before she could change her mind.

"Hi, Mr. Taylor!" Missy said, bouncing into the foyer. "Is Patrick home?"

"Hi, Missy. Yes. He's over there. Playing with his train set, I think."

"Oh, good! Mom, can I go over to see Patrick for a little bit?"

"Missy, Grandma and Grandpa are here, and we're going to be eating soon, so I really think you should just stay home," Shelley said.

"We certainly don't mind if she leaves for a while," said a cool voice. Shelley's mother walked into the foyer from the living room. She looked at John. "Hello." Her pale blue eyes gave him a quick once-over. "I'm Vivian Cochrane, Shelley's mother." She held out her hand.

"John Taylor. I live across the street." John shook her hand. She had a firm grip. Her eyes continued to study him, but it was impossible to tell what she was thinking.

"Can I go then, Mom? Grandma doesn't care," said Missy eagerly.

"No, Missy, I don't think so," Shelley said more firmly. "I don't want you—"

"If you're worried about dinner, I'm not the least bit hungry," her mother said, interrupting. "After all, we had that *enormous* brunch. And you know I never eat two big meals in one day. I don't know why you insisted on cooking tonight. We could have just had something light later on."

Shelley's mouth tightened. Her gaze met John's. "Do you mind if Missy goes over to see Patrick, John?"

"Of course not."

"All right, Missy," she said with an air of resignation. "But I want you home at six. No later. Understand?"

Missy grinned and seconds later she was gone.

Still with that air of resignation, Shelley said, "Before I get that sugar for you, come into the living room and meet my father."

John followed Shelley and her mother into the living room. A tall, slightly stooped man stood when they entered. Shelley introduced them, and John shook Richard's hand, amused to find that his grip wasn't nearly as firm as his wife's. Shelley's father seemed pleasant enough, though. "I've met your son," he told John, "the last time we visited. He's a nice boy."

John smiled. "Thank you. He's a typical eight-year-old, though. Noisy and energetic."

"Yes," Shelley's mother said, "eight-year-olds can be very wearing on the nerves."

John wanted to say that wasn't what he'd meant at all, but Vivian continued talking without giving him a chance to answer.

"It always surprises me that Missy has so little of her father in her," she said.

"Thank God," Shelley muttered.

Vivian gave her daughter a sharp look. "I hope you don't say things like that in your daughter's presence."

Shelley's mouth tightened. "No, Mother, I don't. But believe me, I could say a lot more than that, and it would all be true."

"Shelley, please don't malign Barry to me. You know very well that his mother was my dearest friend until the day she died. It pains me greatly to hear you say ugly things about him, especially when he's never been anything but *wonderful* to your father and me."

Shelley closed her eyes for the briefest of seconds. "How could I forget," she said. "You prefer not to hear the truth."

"Perhaps *you* believe it to be the truth, but I do not." She very deliberately turned to John. "So," she said calmly, just as if the exchange between her and her daughter had never taken place, "how long have you lived across the street?"

"Ten years," John said, thinking that this woman was a real piece of work.

"Oh." She frowned. "That long. But I thought—"

Now it was Shelley's turn to interrupt. "Yes, Mother. John was Cathy's husband."

"You knew Cathy?" he said.

"We met her the year before she died."

John wished now he'd paid more attention when Cathy had talked about Shelley. He would have liked to know what his wife had thought of her parents. Especially mommy dearest.

"Your wife was a lovely woman," Vivian said. "You must miss her."

"Yes," John said. "She was, and I do." Unbelievable how she could be so nasty to her daughter and so friendly to him.

"Would you like to sit down?" Vivian said. "My daughter seems to have completely forgotten her manners today."

"I doubt John wants to stay," Shelley said.

Vivian ignored Shelley. "We were just about to have some coffee. Perhaps you'd like to join us."

John was fascinated by Shelley's mother. He looked at Shelley. He would leave it up to her.

"By all means," she said. "Stay."

"All right." He tried to tell her with his eyes that he was sorry if he'd caused her any discomfort.

"I'll go get the coffee," Shelley said, and left the room.

"Are you and Shelley good friends?" her mother said the moment she was gone.

"Yes, we are." He met Vivian Cochrane's eyes squarely. "Your daughter's a really nice person. I like her very much."

"Shelley's our youngest," Richard Cochrane said.

"You have one other daughter?" John said politely, remembering that Shelley had mentioned an older sister.

"Yes," Vivian chimed in. "Suzanne." She was suddenly very animated. "You've probably seen her photo dozens of times. She's very beautiful. She was modeling for the Fiske Agency by the time she was fifteen. At sixteen, she was chosen to be the Palmer Girl, a place she held for several years." Her voice rang with pride.

"Really?" John tried to think what the Palmer Girl might be.

"You mean Shelley hasn't told you?"

"Hasn't told him what?" Shelley said, entering the room carrying a tray laden with cups of coffee, spoons, sugar and cream. She set it down on the coffee table.

"About Suzanne being the Palmer Girl. Honestly, Shelley, any other woman would be bursting at the seams if she had a family member as successful as Suzanne."

"I guess the subject never came up," Shelley said mildly.

"What exactly is a Palmer Girl?" John said, hoping to sidetrack Shelley's mother.

Vivian smiled happily. "Palmer is a company that makes cosmetics for teens, and for years they've picked the most beautiful models to represent them in their national campaigns. Suzanne was probably one of the most successful of all the Palmer Girls." She looked at Shelley, who had finally sat down. "I still can't *believe* you aren't proud of your sister."

"You do realize, don't you, Mother," Shelley said after a long moment, "that it's been more than twelve years since Suzanne did any modeling at all? And frankly, even if I'd thought to mention her former career, I don't think John's interested."

"Not interested!" Vivian said. "How could anyone not be interested? Why, your sister is famous. Of course, he's interested." She gave John a pained look. "It saddens me to say this, but Shelley has always been jealous of Suzanne, even though she refuses to admit it."

"I never got that idea," John said hurriedly. God, what was wrong with this woman? He couldn't imagine his mother even saying something like that about one of her children, let alone in their presence. "But then, I've never given Shelley much of a chance to talk about her family. I've got a big one of my own, you see, and one of them's kind of famous, herself."

Shelley avoided his eyes. Her cheeks had two pink spots right in the middle. He didn't blame her for being angry. The miracle was that it had taken this long. He'd have been ready to strangle her mother over the Barry comments. Vivian Cochrane was either totally clueless or downright mean. He was afraid it was the latter.

"Oh?" Vivian said. "And who might that be?"

"My sister-in-law. Clem Bennelli. She's a reporter for WNN."

Vivian sniffed. "I'm afraid I've never heard of her." Her tone said someone who was merely a reporter couldn't compare to her daughter.

"I have," Richard Cochrane said. "She's good."

"She's darned good," John said. "She's married to my older brother, Luke."

"Suzanne was married to a baron," Vivian said. "Did Shelley tell you *that?*"

"No, Mother," Shelley said tightly, "I'm afraid I didn't. Suzanne doesn't dominate my every waking thought the way she does yours."

Vivian permitted herself a small, satisfied smile. Her pale blue gaze met John's. *See?* it said. *I told you she was jealous.*

John was a civilized man who had been brought up to respect his elders, but because he cared deeply for Shelley and had finally admitted it to himself, he wished he could cut Vivian Cochrane down to size. He knew Shelley was angry and hurt and embarrassed. Unfortunately, there wasn't much he could do without making things worse for her and, possibly, for both of them. Although he wasn't sure if he and Shelley had any kind of future together, he would hate to alienate her mother just yet. Better to try to smooth things over if he could.

But now he understood Shelley a lot better than he had. No wonder she got so defensive when there was even a hint of criticism directed her way. He was deeply ashamed of the way he'd acted toward her in the past.

He forced a casual chuckle. "Shelley hasn't got a jealous bone in her body," he said. "Besides, she has no reason to be jealous. She's very successful on her own. Has she told you about being offered a manager's position with her agency?"

"No, she hasn't," Richard Cochrane said.

John waited for one or the other of them to encourage their daughter to do so, and when neither parent did, he knew they weren't going to. Worse, he knew they weren't interested. It was getting harder and harder to sit here and listen to them. What was wrong with these people? Didn't they realize they had a wonderful daughter in Shelley? Someone they should be proud of. Someone who hadn't relied on the way she looked to make something of herself? Someone who had worked hard against adversity?

His gaze swung to meet Shelley's. She shrugged. Her body language said she didn't care.

John knew otherwise. He saw the hurt in the depths of her eyes. He wished with all his heart he could get up and enfold her into his arms. He wanted to protect her from these people. He wanted to protect her from everyone and everything that might harm her.

In that moment, he made himself a promise. He didn't know if they had a future together or not. But no matter what happened between them, he would never, ever, knowingly do or say anything to hurt her. She had been hurt enough.

About eleven that night, a few minutes after Shelley had shut off her bedside lamp, the phone rang.

She snatched it up before it could awaken Missy or her parents, who had retired before ten.

"Shelley? I didn't wake you, did I?"

It was John.

"No. You didn't wake me."

"I've been thinking about you ever since I left your house today."

She closed her eyes. There was a tight little ball of pain in her chest. She was mortified that he'd seen the way her mother delighted in belittling her.

"Shelley?" His voice was soft, concerned. "Listen, I want you to know something."

"What?" she whispered.

"I think you're terrific. I think you stack up against anyone. And I think you should tell your mother to go suck eggs."

Shelley started to laugh even as her eyes filled with tears. "Thanks," she finally managed to say.

"Hey, are you okay?"

"Yes." She was surprised to find she meant it. With a few words, he'd even managed to make the pain in her chest disappear.

"I've been thinking about our conversation the other day."

"I have, too." She held her breath, suddenly terribly afraid he was going to say they should forget about what had happened between them.

"I don't know if we have a future together or not," he continued, "but I sure would hate not to try."

Shelley slowly expelled her breath. "Me, too, but—" She swallowed. "I—I'm scared."

"So am I," he said.

She hesitated, then decided if this relationship was to succeed, there had to be total honesty between them. "I'm afraid of being hurt."

"Everyone's afraid of being hurt," he said.

Was that true? Did he have the same fears she had? Shelley didn't see how he could. She didn't see how anyone could.

"It's got to be your decision," he said. "I'm not going to push you to do something you don't want to do."

Okay, so she was scared. But what was the alternative? Never loving anyone? Never trusting anyone? Did she want to spend the rest of her life afraid of committing because she might get hurt? She remembered the night she'd stood at her window and looked across the street. She remembered how she'd decided it was better to have had what John and Cathy had and lose it than to never have had it at all.

I've never had it at all. And unless I take a chance, I never will have it....

Shelley took a deep breath. "I want to try, John."

"You're sure?"

She smiled. "Yes. Very sure."

It was after midnight before John told Shelley good-night. He had thought he wouldn't be able to sleep, but he fell asleep almost immediately and awoke early, refreshed and filled with the kind of excitement and anticipation he hadn't felt in a long time.

He pulled on his sweats and went for a long run. When he got back to the house, the first blush of dawn tinted the eastern sky. He glanced over at Shelley's before going in his back door. Her parents' car was covered with morning mist. He could see lights on inside.

The rich smell of brewing coffee greeted him as he entered the kitchen. Froggie looked up from the morning paper. "'Morning. Have a good run?"

"Good morning. Yes, I had a fine run." John walked over to the cupboard and took out a mug, then poured himself coffee. "I'm glad you're up. I wanted to ask you something."

"Okay."

"I, uh, was wondering if you'd mind watching the kids on your own this coming weekend, and, uh, Missy, too. I, uh..." Good grief, he was stammering like a teenager! "I want to take Shelley to Galveston for the weekend."

Froggie's face lit up in a delighted smile. "Well, thank goodness! I was beginning to think you were *never* going to come to your senses."

"I take it that means you'll do it," he said dryly.

"Gladly."

Shelley said a relieved goodbye to her parents early Monday morning. As her mother and then her father gave her a perfunctory hug, she told herself that this was the last time she would kill herself trying to please them. The episode the day before, when her mother purposely tried to belittle and embarrass her in front of John, had finally and irrevocably shown Shelley that no matter what she did or how she tried or what she accomplished, her mother, in particular, would never approve of her.

So be it, she thought. Like Barry, they were throwing away something wonderful, but it was their choice and their loss.

Her eyes were dry when their car pulled out of the driveway. From now on, she was looking forward.

As Friday rolled closer, Shelley got more and more nervous. When John had suggested they go away together for the weekend, she'd thought it was a wonderful idea. After all, it would be pretty hard to have any kind of intimate relationship otherwise. It wasn't as if she and John lived alone. She could hardly stay over at his house, and he could hardly stay over at her house.

The trouble was, planning to become intimate required too much thinking. And thinking meant that all of Shelley's buried insecurities bubbled to the surface.

Barry had always told her she was lousy in bed. He'd said she wasn't sexy. He'd said she didn't turn him on. He'd said she had no idea how to please a man.

After their divorce, she'd told herself that the things Barry said were said to keep her in her place. That they weren't true. That if she'd been with a man who had made her feel loved, she would have been different.

What if he was right?

What if John were disappointed in her?

Shelley knew he and Cathy had had a good sex life. Cathy hadn't said so, in so many words, but it was obvious by the way she talked. That look she would get in her eyes. That tiny, secretive smile.

John couldn't help but make comparisons.

What if Shelley simply didn't measure up?

All these questions, all these doubts, plagued her the entire week until she was on the verge of calling the trip off. But how could she do that?

On Thursday, she confessed her fears to Linda.

"Oh, Shelley, Barry is a jerk. You know that. He said all those things to keep you beaten down."

"I know, but—"

"But nothing! Don't you *dare* let him ruin this for you by believing *any* of it!"

Shelley subsided into silence. She knew Linda was right. But she couldn't help how she felt. "I'm still scared, Linda," she said in a small voice. "I don't want to disappoint John."

"Listen, if it'll give you more confidence, go buy this book. It's about discovering the joys of sex, and it'll give you some great pointers. Oh, and be sure and get some sexy underwear."

That afternoon, on her way home from work, feeling foolish but determined, Shelley took Linda's advice and stopped at one of the big, anonymous bookstores. Then she visited Victoria's Secret.

That night, after Missy went to bed, Shelley read the book she'd bought from cover to cover. Several times she blushed, but she kept reading. When she was finished, she decided she must be the most inexperienced thirty-one-year-old woman in America.

Unfortunately, the book had done nothing to banish her nervousness. If anything, it made her feel even more doubtful. If that book was any indication, she was woefully unprepared to satisfy a man.

What if she was such a dud, and John was so disappointed in her, that he never wanted to see her again? The thought made her feel hollow inside. She told herself to quit thinking such negative thoughts. That wouldn't happen. John wasn't like that.

But what if it *does* happen? that ugly little gnome of self-doubt persisted. What are you going to do then?

"It won't!" she said aloud. "But if, for some stupid reason, it does, then I'll say goodbye and good riddance to John, because he won't be the man I thought he was."

John had planned to take Shelley to one of the nice hotels in Galveston, but after giving it some thought, he realized she would probably be more comfortable if they had complete privacy. So he called a rental agent recommended by his brother, Matthew, and rented a beachfront condo instead.

The condo was small and luxurious, with sliding glass doors opening from both the living room and bedroom onto a small, private balcony.

The first thing Shelley did when they got there was open the doors and walk outside. John knew she was nervous. It was obvious from the way she'd acted ever since they left Houston. Shelley was not the hyper, overtalkative type, but she'd talked nonstop during the entire hour and a half drive, almost as if she were afraid that if she stopped talking, she might have to think. And if she allowed herself to think, she might panic.

Then, once they'd reached Galveston and were driving along Seawall Boulevard toward the condo, she'd fallen silent, and she'd avoided his eyes.

John put down their two bags and followed her onto the balcony. It was cool and cloudy, with a stiff breeze that had raised whitecaps on the surface of the Gulf. The water looked inky and mysterious. The smell of the sea was everywhere.

John slipped his hand around her waist. He felt the tremor rippling through her body. Tenderness welled in his throat. Scared. She was scared spitless. He knew he would have to go slowly and be very, very patient.

"Why don't we unpack and hang up our things, then go in search of a good place to eat?" he said. "I'm starved."

She inclined her head to look at him. "All right."

He smiled down at her. He so wanted to make this woman happy. "Aren't you hungry?"

She laughed a little, ducking her head. "To tell you the truth, I don't think I can eat. I'm too nervous."

He gave her waist a little squeeze and gently turned her to face him. He cupped her face in his hands. "Shelley, I'm going to make you a promise."

Her eyes were luminous.

"I promise you," he said solemnly, "that we will take things slowly and go at the speed that makes you comfortable. I also promise you that I won't do anything you don't want me to do or make you do anything you don't want to do. Okay?"

She swallowed. "O-okay," she whispered.

He smiled. "Now that we've settled that, do you think it would be all right if I kissed you? I really need to kiss you."

She slowly smiled. "It would be more than all right."

As John's lips brushed against hers, then settled more firmly into place, she sighed, and he could feel her body relaxing. He kissed her slowly, not forcing her in any way, and she was the first to touch her tongue to his.

Immediately John's body leapt to life with an urgency and fire he knew he would have to keep contained until she was ready. And yet he couldn't resist tightening his arms around her or allowing his hand to cup her bottom and press her closer.

He could feel an answering fire in her response to him, and he knew there was no reason to worry. They might still have some rough moments. She wouldn't get over her fear so quickly. But things were going to be all right.

They were going to be all right.

He slowly ended the kiss. "I think we'd better go get that food you promised me, don't you?"

Holding hands, they walked back inside.

Chapter Twelve

Shelley decided John was the most thoughtful, considerate, and thoroughly *sweet* man she'd ever known. She knew he was working hard to amuse her and keep her relaxed throughout dinner.

He took her to a well-known seafood restaurant where they both had the stuffed crab—a specialty of the house. They ate a leisurely dinner, drank a little wine, talked about inconsequential subjects, and looked at the view. The clouds had blown away, and the moonlight cast a silvery ribbon across the water.

After a delicious dessert of key lime pie and coffee, they drove back to their condo. As John unlocked the door, Shelley started to get that jittery feeling in her stomach again. As if he sensed a return of her nervousness, John smiled reassuringly as he stood back and let her precede him into the condo. "Remember what I said earlier?"

She nodded.

"Then relax. I'm not going to bite you." His smile turned teasing. "Well, maybe just a little..."

She couldn't help but laugh.

After that, she felt better. But she still felt awkward. What now? she wondered. Just how did people handle the logistics of something like this? After all, it was one thing to have a guy kiss you good-night or something, and have the kiss turn passionate and then kind of naturally evolve into something else. It was quite another to *plan* to have sex. How were they going to get from fully-dressed-just-back-from-dinner to naked-and-in-bed? Even the thought of getting ready for bed with John watching her made her throat go dry and her stomach start playing jumping jacks.

But Shelley needn't have worried. John, as he had all evening, knew just what to say. He took her hand and said, "Why don't we take turns getting ready for bed? While you're using the bedroom and bathroom, I'll just sit out here and watch the news or something."

Shelley smiled gratefully. She couldn't get over the differences between John and Barry. Barry wouldn't have had a clue about her feelings. Of course, Barry was insensitive to anyone's needs other than his own, and John obviously wasn't.

Shelley tried not to dawdle, even though it was tempting to delay what was coming next. If only she didn't feel so inadequate. If only she was confident of her ability to satisfy John. If only she wasn't so afraid of disappointing him.

By the time she had undressed, taken the pins out of her hair and brushed it so that it fell in loose waves to her shoulders, and donned the delicate seafoam chiffon-and-lace nightgown-and-peignoir set she'd bought to wear tonight, her hands were trembling. *I don't know if I can do this. . . .*

She looked at herself in the full-length mirror on the back of the bathroom door. If she hadn't been practically sick with apprehension, she might have laughed. She looked like a scared rabbit, all eyes, ready to bolt the moment anyone made a move in her direction.

She knew she had to get a grip on herself. She took several deep breaths, pinched her cheeks to put some color in them, and lectured herself.

You've never been a coward. Think of everything you've accomplished in the past few years. Think of how you've faced every challenge, determined to be successful. Tonight is no different. Besides, it's not a firing squad you're facing. It's John. Stop acting like an idiot and go out there and knock 'em dead!

She actually managed a smile at her foolishness, then slowly walked out into the living room.

John stood in front of the TV set with the remote control in his hand. At her approach, he turned. Their eyes met. His slowly darkened as his gaze swept her. When he spoke, his voice was husky. "I've never seen your hair down before."

Automatically, she touched it.

"You . . . you look beautiful."

The pulse in Shelley's throat fluttered. "I—I just wanted to tell you that I'm finished, and if you want to go in . . ."

He turned off the TV, put the remote control down, and walked toward her.

Shelley was mesmerized by the expression on his face.

He put his hands on her shoulders. For a long moment, they simply looked into each other's eyes. It was so quiet, Shelley wondered if he could hear her heart beating. Finally, he took her hand. She didn't resist as he led her back to the bedroom.

Shelley had already turned down the big queen-sized bed and opened the patio doors. The sound of the murmuring sea, punctuated by an occasional sea gull's squawk, drifted into the room. John walked her over to the bed and sat her on the edge. "Now don't go anywhere," he said softly. "I'll be right back."

In the five or so minutes it took him to undress and put on black silk pajama bottoms and brush his teeth and whatever else he did in the bathroom, Shelley did deep-breathing exercises and told herself there was no reason to hyperventilate, that at this very moment there were probably thousands of couples all over the world who were making love.

"And having fun doing it, too," she muttered, disgusted with herself.

"Are you talking to me?" John said, emerging from the bathroom.

Shelley's heart skipped. Wow, she thought. John dressed was attractive and sexy. John in low-slung pajama bottoms and bare chest was gorgeous. She laughed self-consciously. "No, you caught me. I was talking to myself."

"You know what they say about people who talk to themselves, don't you?" He sat down beside her.

"No. What do they say?"

"Well . . ." His eyes twinkled. "They say that people who talk to themselves are great in bed."

Shelley laughed, and once again some of her tension faded. "Do *you* talk to yourself?"

He brushed his lips against her ear. "Oh, yes. All the time."

Shelley shivered. His hand crept around her. She could feel its warmth through the thin fabric of her gown and peignoir. Her breathing escalated as he continued to nuzzle against her ear, then trailed his lips lower to the side of her throat. He slowly untied the ribbons holding the peignoir together and it parted, revealing the low-cut gown and the swells of Shelley's breasts.

With the pads of his fingers, he traced the line of her gown, then lowered his head and kissed her throat and the exposed skin of her breasts. Shelley closed her eyes. Her heart beat harder.

"You're so beautiful, Shelley," he whispered. He continued to kiss her and touch her with the lightest of strokes. "So very beautiful."

"I—I'm not."

"Oh, yes. Yes, you are . . ."

With his thumb, he gently rubbed her nipple. She moaned as it peaked. "Do you like that?" he said, his voice a rough murmur against her skin.

"I—"

"Do you?" he said insistently.

She gasped as a sensation that was half pleasure, half pain, arced through her. "Yes. Yes."

He kissed her then. A slow, almost unbearably delicate kiss. A kiss that tasted and teased and tormented.

And then, very gently, he pulled her to her feet. Slowly, he removed her peignoir and let it slip from her shoulders to the floor. Looking deep into her eyes, he said, "Are you still afraid?"

"I can't help it. It's . . . it's been a long time."

"It's been a long time for me, too."

He held her and kissed her at length. Then he switched off the bedside lamp so that the room was only illuminated by moonlight, and they got into the bed. He seemed to know instinctively that she didn't want to take off her gown or have him remove his pajamas—not just yet.

After that, everything was fine. Everything was more than fine. Everything was thrilling and wonderful and exciting and not scary at all.

When he lifted her gown and said, "Why don't we get rid of this?" she was ready.

Even then he was true to his word. He didn't try to hurry her. His patience paid dividends, for Shelley finally stopped thinking about what was happening and just gave herself up to it. His hands, his tongue, his mouth—all worked their magic, giving her the most exquisite pleasure.

Eventually, she began to touch him, too. At first her attempts were shy and awkward, but they became more sure when he indicated how much he liked what she was doing. His pleasure gave her even more confidence, and she remembered some of the things she'd read about how to please a man. She smiled when he groaned deep in his throat. His reaction made her feel powerful, and she liked the feeling.

He stopped further experimentation by stilling her hands and kissing her deeply. Then he rolled her over and fitted himself up against her, her back to his front, spoon-fashion. Now he was back in control, but this time, Shelley reveled in the sensations. She could feel his arousal against her bottom, his breath and lips against her neck, his hands moving against her skin.

He stroked her until every inch of her felt alive and tingling. His hands moved lower and lower until finally, his fingers delved between her legs.

Shelley's insides turned to liquid heat. Her blood raced through her veins. She moaned as he found her core, the spot that throbbed with a life of its own. His fingers moved in a slow circle.

Shelley squeezed her eyes shut. Her body tensed as the heat built in intensity. She whimpered. She could no longer control it. It threatened to erupt. She twisted, her head thrashing from side to side.

"Shh," he said.

"I can't . . . I can't . . ."

"Yes," he said, "yes. Let yourself go."

And then, in a firestorm of sensation, she was exploding around his hand, spasms of pleasure shuddering through her body. Even then, he refused to let her go. He kept his hand there, in the center of the fire, holding her, continuing to apply pressure, and let her experience the minieruptions that followed. Completely spent, feeling boneless and weak, she collapsed against him. Her heart still pumped madly.

He held her, kissing her neck and her shoulder, caressing her waist, her hip, her thigh.

She sighed. Gradually, her heartbeat slowed.

He pressed her closer, laying his hand against the flat of her stomach. The other hand cupped her breast and gently squeezed. Her nipples responded immediately.

Suddenly she was very aware of his arousal pushing against her—hard and hot.

His hand crept lower.

She held her breath.

Once again, her body tensed as his fingers explored and teased. Once again, she could feel herself slowly climbing higher, getting closer and closer to the top of the mountain. She could feel the lavalike heat bubbling inside, waiting for the moment of release. Her breath came faster and faster. "John," she moaned.

And finally, finally, he turned her. Shelley forgot to be afraid. She forgot everything but this man and this moment and the passion and need burning brightly inside her. She opened herself to him and marveled at how he filled her up, how he seemed to belong, how completely and totally right this was.

This time they climaxed together, within seconds of each other. And this time, her thoughts were with him instead of herself, and when he cried out, she was filled with happiness and pride.

She knew then that no matter what happened, she'd been right. It was better to have experienced this and risk the possibility of losing it than never to have experienced it at all.

"I've missed this," John said later. She was lying in John's arms, and he was lazily caressing her. "And I don't mean just the sex. I mean sharing a bed, being

close, waking up in the morning and knowing someone who cares about you is there.''

Shelley smiled. She was happier than any person
had a right to be. ''I was afraid I'd disappoint you,
you know.''

''Disappoint me!'' He kissed the tip of her nose.
''Why would you think that?''

''Well, it had been such a long time, and I . . . I was
never any good at sex.''

''Shelley . . .'' He tipped her face up.

''Well, I *wasn't!* You . . .'' She swallowed. ''You're
so different from Barry. He . . . he never . . .'' Her voice
trailed off. She didn't want to talk about Barry. She
didn't want those old memories to spoil this night.

''He never what?'' John said softly.

She shook her head. ''No. Let's not talk about it.''

''Come on, Shelley. Tell me. I want you to feel you
can tell me anything.''

She sighed. ''Barry . . . he never seemed to think
about whether or not I was enjoying our lovemaking.'' She stopped. This was so hard. She wasn't sure
she could say this. ''In all the years we were married,
he never once did . . . what you did tonight.''

John frowned. ''I'm not sure I understand.''

She drew circles on his chest so she wouldn't have to
look at him. ''You know. Touched me like that. I
never knew I could feel like that. And even if I had, I
would have . . . felt guilty.''

''But why?''

''Because it seems selfish. I mean, it couldn't have
been much fun for you.''

''Listen to me,'' he said, tipping her face up so he
could look into her eyes. ''I don't ever want to hear

you say something like that again. You were not being selfish. I liked making you feel that way. It turned me on and made my own pleasure that much stronger.''

"It did?"

He smiled. "Oh boy. Did it ever."

Now she smiled, too. "Then why don't we do it again?"

Much later, after they'd made love a second time—which was almost better than the first time, even though Shelley would never have believed anything could be—and after they'd slept awhile, they lay in the dark and talked some more.

"I'd like to get married again," John said.

The funniest feeling slid into Shelley's chest.

"Have you ever thought about getting married again?" he continued.

"No." She fell silent for a few seconds. "But maybe now I will."

Saturday morning they slept late, then had a leisurely breakfast at a nearby café, after which they took a long walk along the beach.

The water looked as if it were sprinkled with diamond dust as it sparkled under the bright November sun. The sky was a deep, clear blue and the air was cool and smelled wonderfully fresh and clean.

They walked for a long time, then sat on a dune and watched the few surfers and the occasional fisherman.

Shelley scooped up some sand and let it trickle through her fingers. The sun felt warm on her back.

She couldn't remember ever feeling so relaxed and replete or so aware of her physical self.

"You know," she said, "when I was young, the only thing I ever wanted was to get married and have a bunch of kids. Instead, I'm divorced, I'm working at a career, and Missy's an only child."

John put his arm around her.

She looked up. Their eyes met.

"Maybe we can do something about that," he said.

Saturday afternoon they climbed into bed and made love again. Then they slept.

At five o'clock, John awakened, but Shelley still slept. He smiled tenderly as he looked at her. She looked younger and more vulnerable than he'd ever seen her, with no makeup, her skin flushed and rosy not only from the sun but from their lovemaking, and her hair tumbled about her. She lay on her side, her mouth open slightly, her chest rising and falling slowly. The sheet and blanket half covered her, leaving her arms and shoulders and half of one breast bare.

John leaned over and kissed her cheek. She stirred and murmured, then settled back into sleep.

He took a shower, thinking about how good the weekend had been so far. It was everything he'd hoped for and more. Shelley was everything he'd hoped for and more.

And their lovemaking . . .

He smiled.

The lovemaking was incredibly satisfying. It was also completely different from the way he'd been with Cathy, and for this, he was very grateful.

He was also hopeful. What Shelley had said earlier today about always having wanted to be a home-maker and the mother of a bunch of kids had made him think their goals and aspirations weren't as far apart as he'd originally believed.

Maybe, in time, she would trust him enough to believe that he would love her and take care of her and never let her down the way her ex-husband had. And maybe, just maybe, then she'd be willing to give up her career and be the kind of wife he wanted and needed.

The future looked promising and filled with possibilities.

And in the meantime, there was tonight....

Saturday night John took her to dinner at a small French restaurant on the Strand. They ate tender veal and fresh asparagus with hollandaise sauce and tiny new potatoes drenched in butter and herbs, accompanied by a crisp white wine and hot bread. Afterward, John talked her into trying the sinfully rich chocolate cake with fudge sauce. The coffee was dark and strong and a perfect ending to the perfect dinner.

Later, they went to a newly opened supper club. John explained that the club was an attempt to re-create the glory days of Galveston prior to and during World War II, when gambling was legal and people flocked to the island in droves.

They danced to the music of a small combo. John wasn't a particularly skillful dancer, but what he lacked in technique he made up for in enthusiasm and the wisdom to keep it simple.

Shelley loved being close to him. Loved having him hold her in his arms, his breath feathering her ear. Loved the feel of his body against hers, moving slowly. She felt completely sensitized to his touch and his smell and completely aware of her own sexuality.

She knew and he knew that later they would go back to their bedroom and, in the glow of the moonlight, make love again. Her body shimmered with a delicious tension, but she felt no hurry to appease it. She knew by now that the building tension would only intensify her pleasure.

A little after midnight, they headed back to the condo. If anything, their lovemaking was even better than it had been before. Afterward, they slept deeply and contentedly in each other's arms.

Sunday morning they again had a leisurely breakfast. And then it was time to pack up and head home.

"I hate to leave," Shelley said. "This weekend was perfect." She finished folding the last garment and zipped her suitcase shut.

"I know," John said. He reached for her, drawing her close. "But there'll be more."

Despite his assurances, Shelley felt sad as they crossed the bridge leading back to the mainland and Houston. She hoped John was right. She hoped they could work everything out and build a future together.

But she was afraid.

This past weekend had been wonderful and romantic. But it hadn't been real life. Real life awaited them in Houston. Real life with the children, her job, her insecurities, all John's memories of Cathy, his expectations and Shelley's limitations, and a million and one other things that could interfere.

Could they overcome all of that?

Shelley hoped with all her heart they could.

But she was still afraid.

Chapter Thirteen

John invited Shelley and Missy to spend Thanksgiving with him and his family. Once again, Shelley had mixed emotions and was half-looking forward to something and half-dreading it.

She wanted to meet John's family, but she was afraid that it would only be natural for them to compare her to Cathy. And she was sure, from the way both John and Cathy had talked about them, that the Taylors had adored Cathy. John's mother and all the rest of them probably missed her terribly.

What if they don't like me? What if they think John is crazy? What if they can't imagine what he sees in me? Shelley hated these negative thoughts, but she couldn't seem to rid herself of them.

She had only seen John once since Sunday, when they'd returned from Galveston. They'd had lunch together on Tuesday. But she'd talked to him every day. In fact, yesterday she'd talked to him twice. Once in the morning, when he'd called her at work to tell her what the arrangements were for today, and again last night after the kids were all in bed.

Now it was eleven o'clock Thanksgiving morning, and she and Missy were supposed to be ready by noon, when John and his kids would come for them.

Shelley had insisted on taking something to his mother's, especially after she found out that everyone brought something.

"But Froggie's going to bake pumpkin pies for me, so we *will* be bringing something," John had said.

"I want to bring something, too," Shelley insisted, and when she saw pecans in the supermarket Tuesday, she bought some. Now she had a fragrant, still-cooling pecan pie as her offering.

"When're they coming?" Missy said crossly. She was tired of waiting.

Shelley rolled her eyes. This was at least the fifth time Missy had asked. "Soon. Now quit frowning. Your face might freeze that way."

"Oh, *Mom!*" But Missy grinned.

Shelley smiled back. She thought Missy looked really cute today in a green corduroy pants and sweater combination, but of course, she was prejudiced. John had said casual dress was in order, so Shelley also wore pants, but hers were gray gabardine paired with a red blouse and gray sweater vest.

She wished noon would come faster, too. The longer she had to wait, the more jumpy she became.

Finally, it did.

"I told you you didn't have to bring anything," John said when she and Missy walked out to meet him. But he smiled, and his eyes told her he was very glad to see her.

He looked wonderful, Shelley thought, but then she was prejudiced where he was concerned, too. He wore casual tan pants and a dark brown turtleneck knit shirt. He wore all colors well, Shelley decided. Actually, he did most things well, and some things he did spectacularly.

She told herself not to think about those particular skills in case he might also know how to read minds. Besides, she was nervous enough.

"You'll enjoy my family," he said as they drove off. "So don't worry."

Maybe he *could* read minds! Shelley laughed self-consciously. "I'm not worrying."

He reached over and squeezed her knee. *I know you are,* his gaze said.

It took them about thirty minutes to get to his mother's home, which was in an older area of northwest Houston. Shelley immediately liked the shady, tree-lined street with its traditional-looking two-story homes and large, manicured lawns. There was something very solid and comforting about it.

The Taylor house was red brick with shiny black shutters and white trim. Two huge oak trees shaded the front yard, and a medium-sized cottonwood as well as a small redbud tree—its leaves now faded and yellow—graced the side yard, along with crepe myrtle and a profusion of fall flowers.

Several cars were parked in the driveway and several more lined the curb in front of the house.

"There are a lot of people here," John warned. "You up for this?"

"I'm looking forward to it," Shelley said. *Well, sort of...*

A variety of good smells, roasting turkey, chief among them, assailed them as they walked into the house. The next thirty minutes were a jumble of impressions and a blur of faces in Shelley's mind.

A smiling young blond woman about Shelley's age was the first person to greet them.

"John!" she exclaimed. "Gosh, it's good to see you!"

John grinned. "Hey, little sister..."

They hugged, and Shelley looked on, knowing this was Rebecca, the only female sibling in John's family. Watching John and Rebecca, and the obvious love and affection they shared, caused a little lump to form in Shelley's throat.

Still grinning, John turned to Shelley. "Beck, this is Shelley. Shelley Broome. Shelley, this is my sister." The grin turned mischievous. "You know, the pain in the behind I told you about."

Rebecca punched John's arm playfully. "I'll give you pain in the behind...." Then she smiled at Shelley and extended her hand. "It's very nice to meet you." Her green eyes were friendly and sincere.

"It's nice to meet you, too," Shelley said, liking John's sister immediately. Maybe this afternoon wouldn't be so bad, after all.

After that, Shelley met so many people in so short a space of time, she began to feel a bit shell-shocked.

There were John's brothers: the single ones—Matthew and James, and the married ones—Paul and

Mark and Luke. James, who was in his early twenties, was a resident at a local hospital—Shelley knew that—so he was easy to remember. He looked like John, too, with the same thick dark hair and the same shaped face and body.

"We take after my dad," John said. He laughed. "Except James got all his brains and *I* got all his charm."

"Yeah, *right,*" James said. He winked at Shelley.

Shelley laughed.

Matthew, Paul, Mark, Rebecca, and Luke all looked like their mother, Shelley thought. They were all tall, all thin, and had the same dark blond hair and green eyes.

Luke was also easy to remember, because he was the oldest, and he was married to one of the most interesting-looking and interesting-acting women Shelley had ever met. Shelley liked her instantly.

"My sister-in-law, Clem Bennelli," John said. He dropped his voice to a stage whisper. "She's a *Democrat.*"

Clem's blue eyes sparkled. "And damned proud of it, too."

John smothered a smile.

Shelley didn't even bother to hide hers.

"Clem thinks I'm a Neanderthal," John said.

"Thinks!" Clem put her hand up to her mouth, pretending to hide what she was saying from John. "Shelley, I have to warn you. He thinks all women belong in the kitchen."

Just then Luke walked over to them and slid his arm around his wife's waist. "Is my brother giving you a hard time again?"

"Giving *her* a hard time," John said. "She's giving *me* a hard time. She's a hard woman."

"Not so hard," Luke said, nuzzling his mouth against her forehead. "In fact, some parts of her are downright soft."

Clem smiled and leaned into her husband in a gesture that openly said she loved him, she loved when he kissed her, and she didn't care who knew it.

Once again, Shelley felt a pang of envy. What nice people these were!

Shelley also met Mark's wife, Miranda, who was Clem's younger sister. Shelley liked Miranda, too, but she wasn't as intriguing as Clem. And then there was Molly, Paul's wife. And kids of all sizes and descriptions, including an adorable set of year-old twins who belonged to Clem and Luke.

"Oh, they're so cute!" Shelley said when Clem showed them off. "What're their names?"

"Lucas and Lee Ann," Clem said proudly.

"Missy," Shelley called. "Come on over and see the babies."

Missy oohed and aahed just as much as Shelley did. Little Lee Ann seemed to take a shine to Missy and even sat on her lap for a while, which was sweet to see.

Shelley had been the most worried about meeting John's mother, Lucy, but as soon as the woman said, "Hello, Shelley. We're so pleased to have you here today," Shelley knew it was going to be all right. Lucy Taylor was one of the most down-to-earth, kind, and unintimidating women Shelley had ever met.

She seemed delighted by Shelley's food-offering, too. "Homemade pecan pie!" she said. "That's my absolute favorite. Thank you so much. That was very considerate of you."

"You're welcome," Shelley said. She looked around the kitchen. "Can I help?"

"Everything's pretty much under control," Lucy said. "But you can stay and talk to me while I stir this gravy."

"If you're going to talk woman-talk, I'll leave and go talk to Luke," John said. Then, surprising the heck out of Shelley, he leaned over and kissed her cheek. "Do you mind?"

Shelley felt herself blushing. "N-no, of course not." When her gaze met Lucy's again, she saw that Lucy was smiling.

"I can't tell you how glad I was when John said he was bringing you and your daughter today," Lucy said.

Shelley didn't know what to say, so all she said was, "Thanks."

"We've all been worried about John," Lucy continued, going back to stirring her gravy. "It's hard to lose someone you love, and it seemed to be taking him a long time to get over it."

"Well, Cathy was a pretty special person."

Lucy paused. "You knew Cathy?"

"Yes. Didn't John tell you?"

Lucy shook her head. "No. He just said he wanted to bring a friend today, and that was it." She tasted the gravy, then picked up the saltshaker and added some. "So how did you know Cathy?"

Shelley explained, finishing by saying, "I still miss her a lot."

"You know, that's nice that you were good friends with her. That probably makes things easier for John, because you understand."

Maybe, Shelley thought. But it didn't make things easier for her, because she understood all too well. And even though she and John were getting along well and she knew he cared for her, she was still afraid that comparisons were bound to take place. And Shelley couldn't imagine how she could ever come out on top.

She and Lucy talked for a while longer, then Lucy said, "Okay. The gravy's ready, which means we can eat."

By one o'clock, the entire clan was seated, filling up the dining room and kitchen tables as well as two card tables. Shelley hadn't seen so much food in one place—outside of parties and cafeterias—in her whole life.

In addition to an enormous twenty-five pound turkey and two kinds of dressing—both corn bread and old-fashioned bread dressing—there were cranberry sauce, a cranberry relish that Lucy said had been her mother's recipe, baby peas, creamed pearl onions, fresh green beans, mashed and sweet potatoes, a marinated salad, fruit salad, homemade biscuits, a pineapple-orange three-layer cake, and five different kinds of pies.

Dinner was a noisy affair. People ate and laughed and talked. Kids ate and ran around and got a good-natured scolding and sat down again. Food got spilled on the floor, and mothers got up and down as they tended to their children as well as themselves. The men joked and the women gossiped. Lucy smiled benignly on everyone.

Shelley thought it was absolutely the nicest dinner she'd ever attended. The Taylors were wonderful, every last one of them. They were warm and friendly and she never once felt they were comparing her to Cathy and finding her wanting. She also thought how this was exactly the kind of family and way of life she'd always dreamed of having.

After dinner everyone helped to clean up, including the men.

"Wow," Clem said, poking John in the arm, "even the Neanderthal is helping."

"I don't know why you call me a Neanderthal," John said. "I've *always* helped out at home."

Clem chuckled. "When you are ready to admit that women belong in the work force right along with men, *then* I'll quit calling you a Neanderthal."

"Some women. I'll admit that."

"Any woman," Clem insisted. "Don't you agree, Shelley?"

Shelley smiled. "Any woman who wants to work should be able to," she conceded.

"I agree," his mother said. "I wish I'd had some kind of training. Maybe if I had, I wouldn't have been in such dire straits when your dad died."

John threw up his hands. "I know when I'm beaten."

Luke, who had just brought a stack of dishes in from the dining room, said, "Any time you get in a disagreement with a woman, you're beaten before you start, don't you know that, John?"

Clem gave her husband a dirty look.

Everyone laughed.

After the cleanup, some of the adults watched the pro football game on TV, others went out to the backyard to play badminton, and still others—mostly the women—sat around the dining room table over second cups of coffee. Shelley joined them.

"So you're a real estate agent?" Miranda said.

"Yes."

"I always thought I'd like selling real estate."

"What *do* you do?" Shelley asked.

"I used to work for a travel agency, but since Robin was born, I've stayed home."

"Do you miss working?"

"Sometimes."

"I know you work, Clem. I've seen you on WNN. That must be tough with year-old twins."

Clem nodded. "Especially when I'm sent somewhere they can't go. That's *really* tough." Her eyes softened. "I never realized how attached to the little ones I'd become."

"Who watches the twins for you?"

"We have a full-time nanny," Clem said. "She even travels with us when we're going someplace everyone can go."

Shelley nodded. Of course. How else would they be able to manage?

"What about your little girl, Shelley? Is she in day care?" Lucy asked.

"No. As a matter of fact, Froggie watches her along with John's children. We just live across the street from John."

"Oh. Now everything is clear," Lucy said. "I knew Froggie had started watching the little girl from across the street, but I never put two and two together until now." She smiled at Shelley. "Isn't Froggie terrific?"

"Yes," Shelley said fervently. "And I'm thrilled that she offered to keep Missy. I was really frantic when I found out my sitter was quitting."

"I'll bet," Molly said. "I know how I'd feel if I lost *my* sitter."

Then someone asked John's sister, Rebecca, about her job. "I work for an advertising agency in Cleveland...Ohio," she said, addressing her explanation to Shelley. "I've been there about a year now."

"What do you do there?"

"I'm an account rep. That means I work directly with the customer."

"She's an idea person," her mother said. "Very creative."

Rebecca smiled. "My mother's proud of me."

"Well, she should be," Miranda piped in. "You've done well for yourself."

The talk gradually turned to other subjects, and before Shelley knew it, it was five o'clock and beginning to get dark out. James came into the dining room and kissed his mother's cheek and said goodbye to everyone. "Got a hot date," he explained. "So I'm leaving. Nice to have met you, Shelley. Come around again."

"Are you going out with Jan?" his mother asked. "I was hoping you'd bring her today."

"Nah. Jan and I aren't dating anymore," he said.

"I liked Jan," Lucy said glumly after James left.

"Kiss of death," Rebecca said.

The others laughed. Shelley hoped that wasn't true because she sensed that Lucy liked her, too.

Eventually, it was time to go.

Shelley felt real regret as she said goodbye to everyone. For the first time in her life, she had felt a part of something special, and she hated to see it end.

On the way home, Shelley tried to tell John how much the day had meant to her, but she wondered if he really understood. How could anyone *really* understand when they'd grown up with so much love?

"Wasn't there anyone you felt close to as a child?" John asked quietly.

Shelley smiled. "My Grandmother Cochrane was wonderful. I used to love to go to her house and always begged to stay overnight. It wasn't until I got older that I realized she was the only one in my family—the only one in the entire world, actually—who loved me unconditionally."

In answer, John reached over and squeezed her knee.

"She always sang to me at night. She had this beautiful old spool bed in her guest room, and I always slept there. She'd get me all tucked in, then she'd sit on the side of the bed and sing to me." Shelley swallowed against the lump in her throat as she remembered. "I can never hear the song 'Let Me Call You Sweetheart' without thinking of her." Now she did brush away a tear. "She always called me sweetheart."

"Is she still alive?"

"No. She died when I was fifteen."

For a while, they were silent, lost in their own thoughts. Then John said, "When we get home, how about if you come to my house and we'll put all the kids to bed there? Then we can be alone for a while."

"What about Froggie?"

"She's spending the holidays in Fort Worth with her sister."

So that's what they did. The kids were thrilled, especially Nikki, whose bedroom Missy shared.

"God, I was about to go crazy for wanting to kiss you," John said later, when they'd finally shared several long, passionate kisses in the privacy of the TV room. "And now I'm about to go crazy because I want to make love to you so bad." He slipped his hand inside her blouse, cupping and kneading her breast.

Shelley closed her eyes. She wanted the same thing. But how could they? "John, don't . . . please don't."

"Shelley . . ." He kissed her again, urgently.

Shelley moaned as he took her hand and placed it over him.

"See how much I want you?" he whispered.

She pulled her hand away and stood up. "We can't, John. I can't. The kids are upstairs."

Immediately he was on his feet. He closed his eyes and leaned his forehead against hers. "I'm sorry. I know we can't. I just . . ."

"I know."

"We're going to have to do something about this, Shelley."

"I know," she said again. There was an ache deep inside her. She wanted more than anything to be alone with him. To have him hold her and make love to her the way he had the previous weekend.

He opened his eyes. His smile was wry. "How do you feel about nooners?"

* * *

They actually managed to be alone quite a few times during the weeks between Thanksgiving and Christmas. Froggie urged them to go out at night, offering to baby-sit at least once every week, and sometimes more often.

John took advantage of her generosity.

On the nights she baby-sat, Missy always stayed over at John's house, so that when John and Shelley came home from their dinner or movie, they could go to Shelley's and feel free to make love.

John didn't spend the night, though, as much as he might have liked to. Neither he nor Shelley felt right about him staying, so he always went home.

And once Froggie took all three kids to Discovery Zone for an entire Saturday afternoon, and John and Shelley spent a wickedly wonderful three hours in her bathtub and then in her bed.

"Nooners are pretty spectacular," Shelley said after that particular episode.

John grinned. "How about me? Am I pretty spectacular?"

She frowned. "Some parts of you."

"Which parts?"

She pretended to be annoyed. "Quit fishing for compliments."

He grabbed her wrist. "I'm not letting you go until you tell me which parts."

"How about if I show you?" she said.

"Thought you'd never ask."

During this whole period of time, Froggie beamed at him. One day, when John was feeling especially happy in the afterglow of spending several hours in bed with Shelley the previous night, Froggie said, "Love is wonderful, isn't it?"

"Excuse me?"

Her smile was very cat-that-ate-the-canary. "You heard what I said."

"Yes, Froggie," he said with exaggerated patience, "love is wonderful." He was amused. She obviously approved of him and Shelley and probably had visions of a wedding in his future.

Another time she said, "A person never knows when he'll find love, and when he does, he should grab it, don't you think?"

John just shook his head. Women! They were all such romantics. But even as he thought this, he knew that he agreed with Froggie. When it came right down to it, he was just as much of a romantic as she was. He did think love was wonderful, and he also thought when you found it, you should hold on to it.

He knew it was time to make a decision.

Christmas had always been a difficult holiday for Shelley. But she had high hopes for this year. She and John and the kids were all going to church together Christmas Eve. Then they were going back to John's house to exchange their gifts.

Christmas Day she and Missy were accompanying John to his mother's house, where once again, his entire family would congregate.

Shelley had thought long and hard about a gift for John, finally deciding on a burgundy cashmere sweater that was sinfully expensive and a beautifully bound edition of the poems of Robert Frost, because he'd once mentioned really liking the poem "The Road Not Taken."

Christmas Eve dawned clear and cold—the first real frost of winter. Shelley was glad to see the change in weather. Sometimes Houston could have seventy-degree Christmases, and she'd never liked those. But today the weatherman predicted a high of only fifty, and that night it was supposed to freeze.

Good, she thought happily. She could wear her dark green velvet and Missy could wear her red velvet, and they wouldn't be too warm.

The candlelight service at John's church began at seven. At six-fifteen, as prearranged, Shelley and Missy, gaily wrapped presents in hand, walked across the street.

"Merry Christmas," John said, opening the door.

"Merry Christmas!" Missy said, eyes shining.

"Merry Christmas," Shelley echoed, heart full as she looked into John's eyes.

John wore a navy pin-striped suit and a red tie and looked so handsome it almost hurt to look at him. Patrick was dressed in a suit, too, and Shelley could tell he didn't like it, because he kept pulling at his tie and giving Missy looks that said this was a pain.

Nikki twirled around in her red-and-green plaid taffeta dress, showing off.

At six-thirty, they all trooped off to church.

The service was lovely, Shelley thought. The women's club had done a beautiful job of decorating, using hundreds of red poinsettias banked around the pulpit and dozens and dozens of tiny white lights on the enormous Christmas tree.

It was wonderful to be there with John and the children, just as if they were a family. Several times, Shelley felt John looking at her, and when she looked up to meet his gaze, he smiled. The smile made her feel warm and happy and loved.

When church was over, they went back to John's where a honey ham and potato salad waited for them in the refrigerator. Shelley and John got everything ready together, and a couple of times, when the kids weren't looking, he sneaked a kiss.

Then they all sat down to eat.

Afterward, it was time to exchange their gifts. They went into the living room, and John turned off the lamps so that the only illumination came from the lights on the tree. Christmas carols played softly in the background.

John loved his sweater and the book of poems.

Missy loved her puzzles and video.

Patrick loved his new video game.

Nikki loved her doll.

Then it was Shelley's turn. John handed her a beautifully wrapped box with long gold ribbons. She opened it and parted the tissue paper inside to discover an exquisite pearl-studded music box. When she lifted the lid and heard the strains of "Let Me Call You Sweetheart" she was so touched she could hardly speak.

"You remembered," she whispered.

"I couldn't believe my luck when I found it," he said.

The kids, obviously not appreciating the mushy stuff going on, clamored to go and play Patrick's video game. John looked at Shelley. "Is it okay with you if they play for a while?"

"Sure," Shelley said. "After all, tonight's a special night."

After they were gone, John said, "How about if I get us some glasses of eggnog, then we can just sit here and listen to the music and maybe I can sneak another kiss or two."

Shelley smiled. She was so happy, she thought she might burst.

When John returned with the eggnog, he sat down beside her on the couch. He put the eggnog on the coffee table. "Before we do anything else," he said, "I have something else for you." He reached into his pocket.

Shelley's hand shook as she accepted the small velvet jeweler's box. "John . . ." Her gaze met his.

His eyes were soft and loving as they rested on her face. "Open it."

She swallowed. Wet her lips. And opened the box. Inside was the most beautiful diamond ring she'd ever seen. It was large and round and fired with brilliant light. Shelley could hardly breathe as her gaze met John's once again.

He took her hand. "I love you, Shelley. I want to marry you."

"Oh, John . . ." She was dangerously close to tears.

"Do you love me?" he asked softly, leaning forward to kiss her gently.

"Yes. Yes, I do. Very much." And never more so than tonight.

"Then will you marry me?"

"I—I want to. But—"

He didn't let her finish. Instead, he gathered her into his arms and kissed her. And when he finally released her, he took the ring out of the box and slipped it on her finger.

"I know there are still some things we need to work out," he said, "but as long as you love me, and I love you, that's all that counts, isn't it?"

Chapter Fourteen

Shelley wanted to say yes. She wanted it more than anything. To be John's wife and mother to his children, to be part of his large and loving family, to finally feel as if she belonged—those were powerful incentives.

But something held her back.

"Tell me what's bothering you," John said.

Shelley looked into his eyes. What she saw encouraged her. "The only reason I'm hesitating to say I'll marry you is ... I'm still not sure you're ready to accept me as I am."

"Now why would you say a thing like that?"

She sighed. This was hard. "John, all of my life people have found me lacking. My parents. Barry. Nothing I ever did was right or good enough. They were always comparing me to other people. People I could never live up to. They were always trying to change me and make me something I wasn't. I—I just can't go through that again.''

"But Shelley . . . I'm not like them.''

"I know you're not, but—''

"But what?''

"You've tried to change me, too. You . . . I don't know if you're even aware of it . . . but you've been comparing me to Cathy, and John, I'm *not* Cathy. I'm never going to be Cathy. I'm me. Just me.''

He looked stricken. "Is that what you think? That I want you to be like Cathy?''

"Don't you?'' she said softly.

"No! I . . . okay, I admit I'd like you to stay home and be a full-time wife and mother the way she was, but that's the *only* thing I'd change about you.''

"But John, I *like* my job. It's important to me.''

"I know that now. I realize you still feel you have something to prove, and that's okay. I can live with it.''

Shelley searched his eyes. "You're sure?''

He smiled and kissed the tip of her nose. "Yes, I'm sure. But you won't have to work as hard, will you? After all, the financial pressure will be gone.''

"Noooo . . . I guess I won't. But what if Walter decides to open a branch office like he talked about? And asks me to be its manager? How are you going to feel about that?''

"We'll cross that bridge when we come to it.''

"What if I want to do it? And it means I'll have to put in more hours? Can you live with that, too?''

"Shelley, sweetheart, let's not worry about what ifs, okay? One problem at a time . . . that's my philosophy. Hell, neither of us knows what the future will bring. All kinds of things could happen. We'll deal with them when they do."

"All right. But John, I've got to feel that you're behind me, one hundred percent. That if something is important to me, it will be important to you, too, and you'll support me."

"I am behind you one hundred percent." His eyes softened. "I love you."

Shelley guessed she could be contented with small steps for now. John was trying hard, and gradually, as he saw she wouldn't neglect him or the children simply because she was working, maybe he would start taking giant steps. "I love you, too."

"Does that mean you'll marry me?"

"Oh, John. If...if you really meant what you said, then yes, yes, I'll marry you!"

John told himself that although Shelley's continuing to work after they were married wasn't ideal, it was an acceptable compromise. Secretly, he hoped that after awhile, she wouldn't feel the need to constantly prove herself. Maybe she'd even cut her hours down to part-time. He decided that would be his goal—to build her confidence and trust and gradually wean her away from her job.

They decided they would be married on Valentine's Day. Shelley wanted a traditional wedding in church with their friends and family around them. "I don't know if my parents will show up or not, but I'm going to ask."

"Whatever makes you happy," John said.

So it was settled. They would be married in Shelley's church and Linda would be her maid of honor. John decided he would ask his brother Mark to be his best man, since he was really closer to Mark than his other brothers. And Missy and Patrick and Nikki would all take part in the wedding.

"Missy's going to be so excited," Shelley said.

John grinned. "If those little devils really were matchmaking, they're going to think this was all their doing."

Shelley laughed. "Well, maybe it was."

"Will you feel awkward if I ask Cathy's parents and sister to be there?" John asked. "They're really nice people, and I still feel as if they're family. Hell, they *are* family. They're my kids' grandparents and aunt."

"No, of course not," Shelley said. "I think it's wonderful that you're close to them."

She had that look in her eyes again. The one that told John she was feeling sad because he had so many people who cared about him and she had so few. He put his arms around her and kissed her. "We're going to be good together, you know that, don't you?"

"Yes," she whispered.

"We're lucky because our kids love each other already, so we'll be a real family from the beginning."

"I know."

"So where do you want to go for our honeymoon?" he said, wanting to erase that look from her eyes.

"I don't know. Where do you want to go?"

"I asked you first."

"What choices do I have?"

"No limits. We'll go anywhere you want to go."

The sadness had disappeared. Now her eyes were filled with teasing glints. "Even if I say I want to ride a barge down the Nile?"

He grinned. "Even then."

She thought for a minute. "You know what I'd *really* like to do?"

"What?"

"Go to Italy," she said dreamily. "I've always wanted to go to Italy."

"I've always wanted to go to Italy, too. In fact, Cathy and I had talked—" He broke off awkwardly.

"John..." Shelley laid her hand over his. "It's okay. I loved her, too."

He covered her hand with his and leaned over to kiss her. "I know you did," he said softly.

She reached up and pulled him closer, giving him a lingering kiss that only fueled his appetite and made him want more. But this wasn't the time or the place. The kids were in the next room. Regretfully, he broke the kiss.

"If we're going to Italy," he said, "we'll need a couple of weeks to do it right. Can you get that much time off work?"

"I don't see why not. It's not as if they have to pay me or anything, and I'll make sure I take care of everything before I leave. In fact, when I go back to work after the holidays, I think I'll tell my boss I'd like to have a month off."

Shelley knocked on Walter Shaver's door early on the morning after New Year's.

"C'mon in, Shelley," Walter said. "You're just the person I wanted to see this morning."

She smiled. As the months passed, she liked Walter more and more. She also respected him, which, from a business standpoint, was even more important.

"You look as if the holidays agreed with you," he said as she seated herself.

She smiled. "I had a wonderful holiday." She held up her left hand. "This was a major reason why."

His face broke into a smile. "Who's the lucky fellow?"

"His name is John Taylor, and he's lived across the street from me for the past five years."

They talked for a while about John and Shelley's plans.

"The reason I wanted to talk to you, Walter," she said, "is that I'd like to take a month off—a week before the wedding, then three weeks afterward." She smiled happily. "John's taking me to Italy on our honeymoon."

"That's great. You'll love it there. Lydia and I went to Italy three years ago, and we've been talking about going back ever since." He smiled. "The time off is no problem, especially since you're going to be working very hard when you return."

"Oh?"

"Lydia and I have decided to go ahead with our plans to open two branch offices—one in Clear Lake and one in the Woodlands. We're targeting the first of March in Clear Lake and the first of May for the Woodlands." He smiled. "If you're still interested, we want you to manage the one in the Woodlands."

Shelley's mouth dropped open in delight. So soon! She'd never dreamed this would happen so soon. And the Woodlands! It was one of the fastest-growing planned communities in Texas. "Oh, Walter! Of course, I'm still interested. In fact, I'm *thrilled!*"

They went on to discuss the different ramifications of the new position, including what her salary and benefits would be.

"One of the nice things about this is you'll be working regular hours, Shelley. No more nights. No more weekends. Except occasionally, if there's a crisis or something," he said.

She hadn't even thought about the regular hours aspect. Oh, it was wonderful! Perfect, even. She couldn't wait to tell John. Maybe they could even move out to the Woodlands. Wouldn't that be great? For the first time, she admitted to herself that moving into a new house—one that held no memories of the past, for John or for her—was an enormously appealing idea.

She knew John would never forget Cathy. She didn't want him to. She'd meant what she said. She had loved Cathy, too. But Shelley wanted her life with John to start fresh. She wanted them to build something together, to make new memories.

As she floated out of Walter's office in a fog of excitement and happiness, she decided Walter's decision to open the new office right now was a sign.

From now on, life would only get better.

"What?" John said. "That's impossible!" He was appalled. "Why, you'll be working even longer hours than you do now."

"No, I won't," Shelley said. "Weren't you listening? I'll be working fewer hours, because I won't have to work nights or weekends. It'll be nine to six weekdays only."

"Nine to six," he repeated. "Which really means seven-thirty to seven-thirty. It's going to take you at least that long to get out there in the mornings and home at night. Good Lord, Shelley, that's twelve hours a day! When will we see each other?"

"Oh, John, you're exaggerating. I work more hours than that now, and we still see each other, don't we? Besides, you leave for work by seven and you don't get home until five-thirty or six. Anyway... I was kind of thinking maybe we could move out there."

"Move out there! I don't want to move out there. Then *I'd* have a long commute, and I hate driving. Besides, I can't take the kids away from this house. You know that." He didn't want to leave the house, either. He knew it was irrational, but he felt as if he'd lose Cathy completely if he left the house.

Shelley stared at him. "Why not?"

"Because this is their house. This is where they've always lived. Anyway, Froggie probably wouldn't want to move that far out."

"We could ask her, couldn't we?"

For some reason, John felt guilty, and that made him mad. There was no reason for him to feel guilty. He hadn't done or said anything wrong.

"Look, Shelley, the issue isn't where we're going to live," he said, "the issue is whether you're going to take a job that will mean longer days and a lot more responsibility."

"So what are you saying, John? That I should turn down the manager's job?"

John knew he had to tread cautiously. He cursed Walter Shaver. Why had this had to come up so soon? Why couldn't her boss have waited a year or so, the way he'd originally planned? "No," he said carefully. "I'm not telling you to turn it down. It's just that I think this is going to require some thought, because if you take it, it's going to be tough on both of us."

It was a long time before she answered him. "I thought this issue was already settled. When you asked me to marry you, I asked you how you'd feel if this situation came up, and you said we'd deal with it. I guess I didn't realize that by 'dealing with it' you meant you hoped I'd forget about it. Well, I haven't and I won't. This job means a lot to me, John, and I want to take it. I not only want to take it, I want to know that you're behind me one hundred percent."

He knew he'd disappointed her, but he couldn't help how he felt. "I *am* behind you one hundred percent."

"Then prove it. Tell me that no matter what I do or don't do, you'll support me."

Slowly, he nodded.

He told himself afterward that agreeing with her did not mean he couldn't keep trying to make her see reason. Because what she was proposing to do was impossible. It would never work. Surely she would realize that after awhile. Maybe all it would take was a few weeks of driving back and forth and the long hours she would have to put in to show her.

He would just have to be patient.

Every spare minute during January was taken up with wedding plans and preparations. One of the first orders of business for Shelley was finding a dress. She asked Linda to go with her to pick one out. Linda suggested they first look in a little bridal shop in Old Town Spring where she knew the owner. They paid the shop a visit the first Saturday in January, and Shelley was thrilled to find a dress that Linda and Phyllis, the owner, both declared perfect.

It *was* perfect—a romantic dusty-rose silk taffeta dress with long sleeves and a high neck and a full skirt ending at midcalf. There was even a matching pillbox hat and frothy veil studded with tiny satin rosebuds to go with it.

"You look beautiful," sighed Phyllis. "Just beautiful. What kind of jewelry will you wear?"

"Pearls?" Shelley said.

"Perfect," Phyllis and Linda said.

Another day they shopped for and found dresses in a deep, rich raspberry for Linda and Missy and Nikki to wear that were a perfect complement to Shelley's.

Then came the search for a place to hold the reception. After looking at dozens of prospects, Shelley and John decided on Vargo's, a popular restaurant set in spectacular grounds and overlooking a small lake.

Once that decision was made, they worked on the guest list, adding here, cutting there, until they were satisfied.

By the third week of January, they were almost finished addressing the invitations. When Shelley got home from work on Thursday night, John called to ask her if she wanted to come over and finish up that evening.

"Okay. As soon as I change my clothes, we'll be there."

"I thought we'd just order a pizza for supper," John said.

"Sounds great. Froggie out tonight?"

"Yes. She said she was meeting a friend for dinner."

"Okay. See you soon."

By the time they'd eaten and cleaned up the kitchen and gotten Missy and Patrick settled in with their homework, and Nikki watching a video, it was seven-thirty. John and Shelley went into the dining room and began to work on the invitations. They had almost finished stamping the last stack when Froggie arrived. She came straight into the dining room.

"Hi, Froggie!" Shelley said.

"I've got something to tell you two," she said, eyes shining.

"Must be something important," John said, "because you look like the cat that ate the canary."

"It is important. I'm engaged!" She held out her hand to show them a lovely solitaire sparkling on her ring finger.

"Froggie! I can't believe it! I had no idea!" Shelley exclaimed.

John looked stunned. "When did this happen? I didn't even know you were seeing anyone."

Froggie beamed. "I know. I didn't say anything because I wasn't sure where it was going."

"Who's the lucky man?" Shelley asked. "And how did you meet him?"

"His name is Will Underwood, and I met him bowling. We've been seeing each other for months now." She looked at John. "Didn't you guess? I kept dropping hints about being in love and how a person should grab love when it came along.''

"I thought you were talking about *me*," John said.

Froggie laughed. "Men." She winked at Shelley. "They're really dense, aren't they?"

Shelley grinned.

"When are you getting married?" John asked.

Froggie grimaced. "Well, that's the part I kind of dread telling you, John. We, uh, thought we'd be married the first of March, right after you and Shelley get back from your honeymoon."

John's expression was bewildered. "Why'd you dread telling me?"

Froggie grimaced. "Because that's not all..."

Froggie's tone warned Shelley, so when the words came, they really weren't a surprise.

"The Houston climate is playing havoc with Will's allergies, so after we're married we'll be moving to Arizona."

Later, after Shelley and Missy had gone home and Missy was in bed, John walked over to talk to Shelley. They sat on the couch in her living room, and he put his arm around her. She sighed.

"Alone at last," he said, kissing her, but she could tell his heart wasn't in it.

"You're worried," she said, touching his cheek.

He nodded glumly.

"Me, too. Honestly, just when you think everything is going great, something happens to throw a monkey wrench into your plans. It's going to be awfully tough to find another housekeeper like Froggie."

"There's no way we will. There's only one Froggie. Besides, I don't want some stranger watching our kids. Do you?"

"Well, of course, I'd prefer Froggie, but you have to be practical, John. And I don't see where we really have a choice."

"You could stay home with the kids."

"I have a job," Shelley said patiently. *Don't get mad. He's upset, that's all...*

"You don't need to work."

"I know I don't need to work. Look, I thought we settled this once. What I'm doing is important to me."

He stared at her, unsmiling. "More important than our children?"

"Of course not."

"Well, then ... seems to me that's your answer."

Shelley sighed. Somehow she had to make him see. "Come on, John, it's not as if they're going to be neglected. With the money I was paying for child care added to what you were paying Froggie, why, we should be able to get someone top-notch."

"A top-notch stranger," he said stubbornly.

Shelley could feel her temper simmering. "I think maybe we'd better drop the subject for tonight. Why don't we both sleep on it? Maybe tomorrow we'll have a better perspective."

"I'm not going to change my mind, Shelley."

Oh, she hated that patronizing tone of voice, that implacable I-know-best stance she'd seen too often in her life. "I see. What it comes down to is, I'm going to be the one to have to change, is that it?"

He actually looked pained, as if she were being unreasonable.

"I don't know what the big deal is," he said. "Hell, Shelley, you admitted to me once that all you ever wanted was to stay home and be a wife and mother. Well, now's your chance." His voice softened. "Look, I was willing to go along with your working. I was willing to be patient and wait for you to come to your senses, but now things are different."

Shelley stared at him. She couldn't believe what she was hearing. "You were willing to *go along* with my working? You were willing to *be patient?* To wait for me to *come to my senses?*" she repeated. "Surely you didn't mean that the way it sounded."

"Come on, Shelley, don't get melodramatic."

"Don't get melodramatic! What happened to you backing me one hundred percent? What happened to supporting me in my decisions? Was that all just something you said to placate the little woman? Didn't you mean a word of it?"

John sighed wearily. "Oh, for crying out loud. I meant it when I said it. But surely you realize that this is more important than you needing to prove something. This is the welfare of our children we're talking about. Don't you think it's time you got your priorities straight?"

Shelley jumped up. Her voice was tightly controlled. "All my life people have been criticizing me and my choices. I told you before, I can't live that way anymore. I won't live that way anymore."

"I'm not criticizing you. I'm just pointing out the obvious."

"Showing me where I'm wrong, and you're right."

"In this instance, yes."

Shelley's shoulders slumped wearily. "I thought you were going to be different, John. I really did. But now I see I was wrong." She tugged at the ring on her finger. "I can't marry you."

He stood, too. He tried to take her into his arms. "You don't mean that, Shelley."

"Yes, I do. Unless and until you can accept me as I am and love me without placing conditions on your love, I can't be your wife." She thrust the ring at him. "Now please go. I'm very tired and I want you to leave."

Shelley was trembling inside. She waited for him to say he'd been wrong. She waited for him to say he loved her just the way she was. She waited for him to say she could work or not work, stay home or not stay home—the choice was hers.

He said nothing.

She forced herself to speak around the awful lump in her throat. "Good night, John." She turned and walked into the hall. She heard him coming behind her. She didn't look around.

And then she heard the door open and close.

He was gone.

Chapter Fifteen

Shelley cried herself to sleep. The next morning, her eyes were all red and puffy, and she had a raging headache. Missy noticed.

"What's wrong, Mom? Are you sick?" she said.

Shelley kept her head averted as she measured coffee into the coffeemaker. *Sick? Does heartsick count?* "I think I might be coming down with a cold." She switched the unit on. "Do you want pancakes for breakfast?"

"Okay."

As Shelley mixed up pancake batter, she once again replayed every word of last night's conversation. Completely engrossed in her misery, she didn't realize Missy was talking to her.

"Mom!" Missy said, eyes filled with alarm. "Where's your ring? Why'd you take it off?"

Shelley looked down at her left hand. "I..." She stopped. She didn't know what to say.

"You didn't lose it, did you?" Missy's voice vibrated with concern.

Shelley looked up and met her daughter's eyes. She shook her head slowly. She had thought, after her agonizing night, that she was all cried out. She'd been wrong. Tears clogged her throat again, making it difficult for her to speak. "No, honey, I didn't lose it. I—I gave it back to John."

Missy frowned. "But why?"

"I..." Shelley bit her bottom lip to stop its trembling. "I made a mistake. I thought..." She broke off. "I can't talk about this now, Missy. The engagement is off. I'm not going to marry John."

In the days following the blowup with Shelley, John charged around the house and the office like a caged bear. He was spoiling for a fight. It didn't take long for people to start avoiding him.

John knew they were all talking about him. He hadn't told anyone except Froggie what had happened, and that was only because he'd had no choice.

"Do you want me to mail these invitations for you?" she asked the morning after her startling announcement. In her hand was the stack of stamped, addressed wedding invitations he and Shelley had been working on before his whole world came crashing down around him.

John shook his head. He didn't meet Froggie's eyes.

"But, John, it's less than three weeks before the wedding—"

"There's not going to be any wedding!" he said and stomped off.

A few minutes later, she walked out back where he stood shivering and gazing sightlessly around his winter-barren backyard. She touched his shoulder. "Come on inside, John," she said gently. "It's freezing out here."

"Leave me alone, Froggie." He felt ridiculous, but he couldn't face her. He couldn't talk about it.

"I'm not going to leave you alone, and if you won't come inside, then I guess we'll *both* have to freeze."

John sighed wearily. "Oh, all *right*. You win."

A few minutes later, back in the warm kitchen, she said, "Okay. Why isn't there going to be a wedding?"

"Let's just say Shelley and I have irreconcilable differences and leave it at that, okay?"

"No, it's not okay. What kind of differences?"

John stared at her. He considered telling her it was none of her business. But he figured she was bound to find out what had happened sooner or later. And if she was going to find out anyway, he'd rather tell her himself.

"Oh, John," she said when he'd finished. "You didn't really say all those things to Shelley, did you?"

"Don't *you* start in on me! Hell, Froggie, you know how important it is for kids to feel secure. Especially my kids. I don't want them raised by a succession of baby-sitters. You're different. You're family. You love them."

She gave him a long, thoughtful look. "Tell me something, John," she said slowly. "What if you and Shelley hadn't been engaged? What if I had come to you and told you I was leaving, and there was no option like Shelley in the wings? Wouldn't you have been forced to look for outside help?'' When he didn't answer, she said, ''And what about now? Aren't you in that same boat now? If you and Shelley aren't getting married, you'll have to find a housekeeper or put the kids in day care or something.''

John pressed his lips together.

''So what you've done is made yourself and Shelley miserable for nothing.''

John wanted to tell her she was wrong. He wanted to tell her it wasn't all his fault. But he couldn't get the words out.

Froggie shook her head sadly. ''You know, John, all kids need to feel secure is a loving environment. If your kids see that you and Shelley love each other and them, and they know that each night you'll be coming home, it won't matter if someone else is watching them for a few hours.''

''That isn't the kind of life I want.''

''So you'd rather have a life alone?''

''I've done fine on my own the past three years,'' he said stubbornly.

Froggie sighed. She looked at him for a long moment. ''Pride and stubbornness make very poor companions.''

For the rest of the day, she kept saying things like, ''It's a shame some people are so blind,'' and ''I can't really respect someone who can't admit when he's wrong.''

Finally John lost his temper. ''Mind your own business, Froggie,'' he said through clenched teeth.

She looked at him over her reading glasses. "Oh? It was okay for me to mind your business the past three years when you needed my help, but it's not okay now? Well, pardon me, John, but I calls 'em as I sees 'em, and the simple truth is, you are a fool."

"Mom," Missy said two days later as she was getting ready for school, "when are you and Mr. Taylor gonna make up?"

Shelley pursed her lips. "We're not."

"But why not? Don't you *wanna* marry him?"

"I thought I did."

Missy didn't answer for a moment, and Shelley turned around to look at her. "You know what I think?" she said angrily. "I think you and Mr. Taylor are acting like a couple of kids!" She slammed her lunchbox shut. "I'm leaving. Goodbye."

After she left, Shelley burst into tears.

When Missy arrived at Patrick's house after school that day, she said, "Patrick, we've gotta do something."

A few minutes later, the two of them found Froggie in the kitchen where she had just fixed Nikki a bowl of soup.

"What're we gonna do about Dad and Shelley?" Patrick said. "Do you think they're ever gonna make up?"

Froggie shook her head wearily. "At the rate they're going, it will take some kind of miracle or crisis to make them see the light."

Later, as Missy and Patrick worked on their homework, Missy said, "I've been thinkin' about what Froggie said. You know...about a crisis?"

"Yeah?" Patrick said cautiously.

"What if something bad happened? Something where your dad and my mom had to talk to each other?"

"Like what?"

"Well, I was thinking...what if you and me ran away?"

"Ran away!"

"Shhh," Missy said. "Your Aunt Froggie might hear us."

"But, Missy—"

"We don't have to go far," she said. "And we don't have to stay away long. Just overnight."

"But where would we go?"

"Well, there's that empty house down the street..."

"That house is spooky," Patrick said. He didn't like empty houses.

"Oh, come on, Patrick, don't be a *baby!*"

"I'm not a baby!"

"Yes, you are."

"No, I'm not!" Patrick said.

"Then you'll do it with me?"

Patrick sighed. "Okay. When do you wanna go?"

Shelley was exhausted. And she had a headache. That was nothing new, though. She'd had a headache every day since she and John had broken up.

It had been a week. A long, terrible, miserable, lonely, awful week.

Several times she'd almost called him.

Then she'd thought, what was the point?

She decided she would change her clothes before calling John's house to tell Missy she was home. Since the breakup, Shelley had avoided John's house, even when he wasn't there. She didn't want to have to see or talk to Froggie or face the sad faces of the kids.

Ten minutes later, dressed in her favorite worn jeans and a red University of Houston sweatshirt, she walked out to the kitchen to search out the bottle of aspirin.

The note was propped up in the middle of the kitchen table.

Curious, wondering why on earth Missy had left her a note, Shelley picked it up.

Dear Mom, she read. *I know it's my fault you're mad at Patrick's dad. So I'm running away with Patrick so you won't be mad anymore. Missy.*

Shelley's heart slammed into her chest. She spun around, grabbing for the phone on the wall.

"Froggie," she said when the older woman answered. "This is Shelley. M-may I please speak with Missy?"

"But I thought... isn't she there with you?"

"What do you mean?" Panic careered inside. *Please God, please God...*

"Didn't you call here about thirty minutes ago?"

"No! Why would you think so?"

"Missy told me you'd called and were home and she and Patrick left to go to your house," Froggie said quietly.

"I'm coming right over!" Shelley shouted. She slammed the phone down, grabbed the note, and raced out of the house.

* * *

Patrick had left a note, too. Froggie opened it, even though it was addressed to John. It was identical to the one Missy had left Shelley.

"We've got to call John," Froggie said.

"We've got to call the police!" Shelley said. She'd never been so frightened in her life. She'd been praying for the past ten minutes, bargaining with God, telling Him if only He would keep Missy and Patrick safe, she would do anything, anything...

They called both the police and John. While they were waiting for them to arrive, Shelley called every mother she could think of, then Froggie did the same. The kids weren't at any of the houses.

Froggie had just hung up from her final call when they heard the sound of a car careening into the driveway. "It's John," Froggie said.

A car door slammed, then footsteps pounded toward the back door. John crashed into the house with the force of a small tornado. "How in the hell did this happen?" he shouted.

"Calm down, John," Froggie said. She handed him the note. "I'm very much afraid this is my fault. Earlier today the kids came to me. They were very concerned about the two of you breaking up."

Shelley winced. Her eyes met John's. She saw the same misery and guilt and fear in his eyes that she knew were in hers.

"Anyway," Froggie continued, "they asked me what I thought they could do to get you back together, and I said I didn't know. That it would take a miracle or a crisis for you two to see the light."

"Oh, my God," Shelley said, putting her hand over her mouth.

"Dammit," John swore softly. He ran his hands through his hair. Then he looked around. "Where's Nikki?" Panic threaded his voice.

"She's still napping upstairs," Froggie said.

Shelley saw the relief wash over his face. She felt guilty because she hadn't even thought about Nikki.

By now the police were at the door. John let the two officers in, then Shelley and Froggie told their stories one more time.

One of the officers, a fortyish man with kind brown eyes and curly dark hair, said, "They're probably right around here somewhere. Have you looked around the neighborhood?"

"Not yet," John said. He'd managed to get his panic under control.

"They'll probably show up before dark," the other officer, a bright-faced redhead, said. "They usually do."

Shelley hugged herself. Oh, God, she hoped, she prayed the officers were right. Surely the kids were okay. But newspaper and TV stories of kids who had been picked up by predatory strangers, of kids who had disappeared into thin air, refused to go away.

Please, God, please, God... The words played in her mind, over and over again.

"We'll search the neighborhood," the dark-haired officer said.

"I'll come with you," John said.

"I will, too," Shelley said.

"Why don't you stay here, ma'am?" the red-headed officer said. "In case they call."

John took Shelley's hand. He squeezed it. She bit at her bottom lip to keep it from trembling and forced herself not to cry.

The next hour dragged by. At six-thirty, John and the officers were back. There'd been no sign of Patrick or Missy anywhere. They had knocked on every door, looked in every yard.

And now it was dark.

John didn't know whom he felt worse for—Froggie, who he knew felt responsible; Shelley, who he knew was as scared as he was; or himself.

If only he didn't feel so guilty.

And so scared.

All sorts of horrible stories catapulted through his mind. He tried not to think of them. He kept telling himself the kids would be all right. They *had* to be all right. He would never forgive himself if they weren't.

"It's all my fault," Froggie said, her face showing the strain of the last hour.

"You couldn't have known what they'd do," Shelley said. "No, if it's anyone's fault, it's mine. I knew how upset Missy was." She looked on the verge of tears, and John wanted more than anything to take her into his arms.

"I'm the one who's at fault," John said, looking at Shelley. "I can't tell you how sorry I am." Suddenly, he had to talk to her alone. He walked over to her and put his arm around her shoulder. "Come into the living room."

She let him lead her away without protest. When they were by themselves, he put both arms around her and tucked her head under his chin. He could feel the quivering in her body. "I'm so sorry, Shelley," he said again, kissing the top of her head. "For everything."

"I'm sorry, too," she said brokenly.

He lifted her chin and gave her a tender kiss. He could taste her tears. "I've missed you so much," he whispered.

"And I've missed you."

"I want you to know that I've done a lot of thinking since the night you gave me back my ring. And what I've discovered is that I love you—just the way you are. Whatever makes you happy, makes me happy."

"Oh, John..."

His arms tightened around her. "Froggie was right. I've been such a fool. Can you ever forgive me?"

"I've already forgiven you."

"If we get the kids back—"

"We *will* get the kids back," she said fiercely. "I know we will."

"Will you still marry me then?"

She closed her eyes, leaning her head against his chin. "I want that more than anything in the world."

The officers left at eight o'clock. There was nothing more for them to do there. "We'll get a bulletin out, sir," the dark-haired officer said to John. "Don't worry. They'll turn up. They're probably hiding somewhere that we haven't thought of, that's all."

"I hope you're right," John said.

Shelley didn't know what she'd do if anything bad happened to Missy. She didn't think she could stand it.

"In the meantime, if you think of anything, call us," the officer said.

After they'd gone, Froggie fixed some soup and a grilled cheese sandwich for Nikki, who seemed bewildered by all the commotion. "How about you two?" Froggie asked. "Do you think you could eat something?"

"I can't eat," Shelley said.

"Me, either," John said.

Froggie nodded and sat down next to Nikki at the kitchen table. She stared off into space. Shelley fixed herself a cup of coffee, and John paced back and forth. One by one they looked at the silent phone.

At nine Shelley thought she was going to go crazy. "Where can they *be?*" she cried.

Froggie, who'd had her head buried in her arms, looked up. "I just thought of something!"

"What?" John said.

"The other day Patrick mentioned a house down at the end of the street. He said he thought it was spooky. I guess it's been standing empty for a while."

"I know the one you mean. That funny-looking woman, the one who had a pom-pom flying from the antenna of her car, lived there."

"I remember her!" Shelley said. "The kids were all a little afraid of her."

"Do you think they might be in that house?" Froggie said. "Did you check that house, John?"

"We checked the yard, but the house was dark."

Ten minutes later John and Shelley were knocking on the door of the vacant house. "Patrick! Missy! If you're in there, please say something!"

Shelley peered in the front window. She couldn't see anything except a streak of moonlight. She banged on the glass. "Missy! Missy! Are you in there?"

"I'm going to go around and check all the windows," John said.

"All right."

Just as John rounded the corner of the house with Shelley a few steps behind him, a side window opened and Patrick said, "Dad, here we are."

Relief gushed through Shelley, causing her knees to buckle as John pulled first Patrick and then Missy through the open window. She was too happy to yell at the kids, too thankful that they were all right. She just kept saying, "Oh, thank you, God, thank you."

Missy tumbled into her arms, and Shelley hugged her hard. "Oh, Missy, Missy, you scared us so."

"I'm sorry, Mom. But we didn't know what else to do. You and Patrick's dad weren't talking to each other, and it didn't look like you ever would. When we asked Froggie about it, she said only a crisis would get you back together...so that's when we thought about running away."

"I should give you a good spanking, young man. You scared the life out of us," John said, but he was hugging Patrick hard, too.

"I'm sorry, Dad," Patrick said.

"But did it work? Are you guys back together now?" Missy said.

John chuckled. "Yes, you minx, it worked." He reached for Missy and hugged her, too.

Shelley had a lump in her throat as the four of them, holding hands, walked home.

Froggie's face lit up when she saw them. After more hugging and good-natured scolding, John said he'd better call the police.

Later, as they were all sitting around the kitchen table eating grilled cheese and some of the soup Froggie had made earlier, Patrick said, "We want to be a family, Dad. Me and Nikki, we want Shelley to be our mother." He looked at Missy. "And we don't care if she works. We'll even go to day care if we have to, won't we, Missy?"

"Uh-huh," Missy said. "We don't care. As long as we're all together."

"I know," John said. He put his arm around Shelley. "That's what I want, too."

Shelley smiled at him. Her heart was so full.

He smiled back, then bent his head and kissed her.

Nikki giggled.

Missy and Patrick made thumbs-up signs and cheered.

Froggie beamed.

As John lifted his head and smiled down into her eyes, Shelley knew she finally had nothing left to prove. "You know," she said thoughtfully, "maybe we won't need to find a housekeeper, after all. I might just decide that staying home with you kids is all the job I need or want."

John squeezed her shoulder. "Let's not decide anything right now. I want you to be happy. That's the most important thing."

"No," Shelley corrected him, "the most important thing is that we're all together and that we love each other."

"Hallelujah!" Froggie said.

Missy grinned. "In fairy tales, this is when it says *and they lived happily ever after.*"

* * * * *

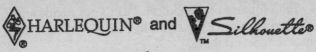

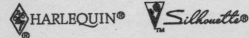

Take 4 bestselling love stories FREE

Plus get a FREE surprise gift!

As seen on TV!
Free Gift Offer

With a Free Gift proof-of-purchase from any Silhouette® book,
you can receive a beautiful cubic zirconia pendant.

This gorgeous marquise-shaped stone is a genuine cubic
zirconia—accented by an 18" gold tone necklace.
(Approximate retail value $19.95)

Send for yours today...
compliments of ▼ *Silhouette*®
TM

To receive your free gift, a cubic zirconia pendant, send us one original proof-of-
purchase, photocopies not accepted, from the back of any Silhouette Romance™,
Silhouette Desire®, Silhouette Special Edition®, Silhouette Intimate Moments®
or Silhouette Yours Truly™ title available in August, September or October at your favorite
retail outlet, together with the Free Gift Certificate, plus a check or money order for
$1.65 U.S./$2.15 CAN. (do not send cash) to cover postage and handling, payable
to Silhouette Free Gift Offer. We will send you the specified gift. Allow 6 to 8 weeks for
delivery. Offer good until October 31, 1996 or while quantities last. Offer valid in the
U.S. and Canada only.

Free Gift Certificate

Name: _____

Address: _____

City: _____ State/Province: _____ Zip/Postal Code: _____

Mail this certificate, one proof-of-purchase and a check or money order for postage
and handling to: SILHOUETTE FREE GIFT OFFER 1996. In the U.S.: 3010 Walden
Avenue, P.O. Box 9077, Buffalo NY 14269-9077. In Canada: P.O. Box 613, Fort Erie,
Ontario L2Z 5X3.

FREE GIFT OFFER   084-KMD

ONE PROOF-OF-PURCHASE

To collect your fabulous FREE GIFT, a cubic zirconia pendant, you must include this
original proof-of-purchase for each gift with the properly completed Free Gift Certificate.

084-KMD

You can run, but you cannot hide...from love.

This August, experience danger, excitement and love on the run with three couples thrown together by life-threatening circumstances.

Enjoy three complete stories by some of your favorite authors—all in one special collection!

THE PRINCESS AND THE PEA
by Kathleen Korbel

IN SAFEKEEPING
by Naomi Horton

FUGITIVE
by Emilie Richards

Available this August wherever books are sold.

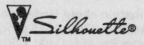

You're About to Become a *Privileged Woman*

Reap the rewards of fabulous free gifts and benefits with proofs-of-purchase from Silhouette and Harlequin books

Pages & Privileges™

It's our way of thanking you for buying our books at your favorite retail stores.

PROOF OF PURCHASE
SSE-PP167
Offer expires October 31, 1996

Pages & Privileges ™

Harlequin and Silhouette—
the most privileged readers in the world!

For more information about Harlequin and Silhouette's PAGES & PRIVILEGES program call the Pages & Privileges Benefits Desk: 1-503-794-2499

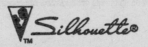

Silhouette®

SSE-PP167